D1473933

WITCH of KEY LIME LANE

DEAD & BREAKFAST #1

Gabrielle Keyes

WITCH OF KEY LIME LANE

ASIN: B097SVDY9L (eBook Edition)
ISBN: 9798543612453 (Print Edition)

Printed and bound in the United States of America
First printing July 2021
Published by Alienhead Press
Miami, FL 33186

GABRIELLE KEYES

*"Life is a series of hellos and goodbyes.
I'm afraid it's time for goodbye again."*

BILLY JOEL

1

1

I know what you're thinking.

You see that internet photo with the woman in her mid-40s, wearing an eerily zen smile and sweats, messy top bun, holding a glass of wine, grinning from ear-to-ear while setting fire to her ex's belongings on the sidewalk, and you think: *Lily Blanchett has lost her bananas.*

And you would be right.

Bananas or marbles, it was not my finest moment.

The headline is usually something like: *Wife of Celebrity Chef Derek Blanchett Holds Breakup Bonfire* (though sometimes they're kind enough to use my name). And if you're lucky, you might see the bonus image of me flipping a bird at Mrs. Napoli, my nosy neighbor who captured the moment and sold the photos to the tabloids.

Ah, good times.

I checked the time on the lasagna. Five more minutes. I poured another glass of pinot noir, as David Bowie wrapped his chonky white and ginger body around my leg, meowing like the world's supply of tuna had ended.

"I've fed you five times today, Bo. Go run a lap."

Nowhere did the articles ever mention how I found out about Derek's secret-squirrel life. Nowhere did they explain how I had to listen in agony to my daughter Emily call from her dorm, crying her eyeballs out, all because she'd gone to dinner with friends and seen her father with another woman and two kids who looked like both of them. How she'd gone up to him, demanding to know who the hell the woman was, only for Derek to confess, in the middle of *P.F. Chang's*, that she and her brother had half-siblings.

They never showed my daughter's tears. Or her therapy bills. Or the hole my son punched in his dorm wall that I had to pay for. No, they only showed Batshit Crazy Lily. Having a bonfire. On the sidewalk of her Long Island home.

I'd held onto his stuff for a year—*a year*—naively wishing the nightmare would go away. Maybe I'd wake up and find Derek home one day, telling me it was all a joke. He never cheated, never fell in love with a redheaded yoga instructor. Things could go back to normal now. Or maybe if I worked hard enough, put in longer hours, more sweat and tears into the restaurant, my life would miraculously resolve itself.

Dumb, I know.

But then, Weasel's marital settlement agreement finally arrived on my doorstep, decreeing several injustices. One, that he wouldn't pay child support of any kind. The kids were adults now, and he had little ones to worry about. Weasel also declared his plan to take our restaurant, the career baby we'd *both* cultivated and poured our hearts into, on the idea that we wouldn't be able to work in the same kitchen together anymore.

And finally, because he'd bought this house fifteen years ago under his name only (I never thought I'd have to add my name to the deed—I thought our marriage was *forever*), he'd be taking the house as well.

That was the final blow. I knew he was taking revenge for my getting a restraining order put against him, which made him lose his TV show, but what else was I supposed to do after he pinned me to the kitchen fridge in anger? All because I compared him to his violent father during an argument. Well, it was true. I'd never seen him act that way before. The agreement also said I should pay for the kids' college tuition myself, since Emily and Chase had stopped talking to him anyway.

So, to summarize: no restaurant, no house, no income, and only a three-month savings off which to live. As if any of this were my fault. Ask Derek, however, and he'd tell you it was me—my emotional (and physical) distance from him, my workaholic ways—that *made* him cheat.

Of course. Everything was always my fault.

So, yeah, I snapped. Burning the last of his shirts, TV awards, and boxers had been a bit dramatic, but damn did it feel good.

Even then, it was hard to let go. As much as the world made it seem like getting over Weasel should be easy, or like my therapist said, it was unhealthy to keep giving him so much of my "energy," I couldn't stop thinking about him. Couldn't stop engaging in text wars, couldn't stop stalking him and his girlfriend on social media, couldn't move on with my life.

I mean, listen. For twenty-two years, Derek had been my life. I gave him *everything*. I hadn't insisted my name go on the house, because I didn't live in fear of losing him. That had been a mistake. I gave up my last name for him. I moved to New York City for him. I kept our restaurant in order for him, so he could have fun as the host of *Blanchett's BBQ*

Challenge. And for a passionate restauranteur like me, losing *Chelsea Garden Grill* was just as devastating.

The oven timer buzzed. Bowie took a seat at the counter stool, and my phone rang—my mother—all at the same time. I groaned and took a long sip of wine. "Hi, Mom," I answered.

"Hi, Lily. It's Mom."

"I know. I just said, 'Hi, Mom.'"

"Don't be aggressive, darling."

"Mom, I'd know your voice in my sleep. You're my mother."

"Good, I'm glad. Listen…your Aunt Sylvie said you can use her cottage."

"Cottage?"

"Her house down in the Keys."

"In Florida?"

"Yes, the only house she's ever had. The one we used to stay at when you kids were little."

I knew which house she meant, but I didn't know Aunt Sylvie still owned it. For the last thirteen years, my elderly aunt had lived in an assisted living facility in Tampa. Her tiny beachfront home we used to visit as a family off Islamorada had long become a foggy, sun-soaked memory. As an ambitious 12-year-old, I always imagined her house to be my very own home away from home.

"I never asked if I could use her cottage, Mom." I pulled a block of aged Parmigiano-Reggiano from the fridge.

"I know that, Lily. I asked for you."

"Why would you do that without asking me first?"

Her sigh leaked into my ear. "Because you need to get away for a while, honey. I think the fresh ocean air will do you good."

"Mom, I'm not crazy. The tabloids are just making me seem that way. It's called sensationalism. It sells magazines. You know this."

"It's a cry for help, darling."

"No, Mom." My blood boiled, an instant symptom of discussions with her sometimes. "Need I remind you that burning his stuff on the sidewalk was actually a bold and healthy move for me? He's taken enough advantage of me. I had to send the signal that I won't be bullied or humiliated anymore."

"Honey, a smoke signal was the only signal it sent. And the fire department was nice enough to let you off with a warning. You got lucky."

"Lucky?? Tell me why are you calling again?" I lifted the lasagna out of the oven and plopped it on the counter. Frozen Kirkland brand. I'd reached a new low.

"I told you. Your Aunt Sylvie—"

"Yes, got it." I clipped fresh basil from the potted herbs by my window. It may have been frozen lasagna, but presentation is everything. "Aunt Sylvie said I could use her old house if I wanted."

"Right, and since you won't be working at the *Garden Grill* anymore—"

"I never said I won't be working there anymore, Mom. That's what Derek's agreement proposed, but I don't have to accept his terms. I can fight it, and I intend to."

"Why? Do you really want to work in the same kitchen space as your ex-husband who cheated on you with a woman he met on Limber—"

"Tinder, Mom."

"Do you really want to see him every day? Bump into him constantly? While holding a chopping knife? With a meat grinder nearby? Lily, I'm a tad concerned."

"He won't be there all the time, and it's not just *his* restaurant, Mom." I rolled up the basil for the chiffonade. "We built it from the ground up *together*. We became the #1 Debut Restaurant of Greenwich Village less than three years after Grand Opening." I scraped the basil shreds aside and slammed the knife onto the cutting board. "We got a cooking show on the *Cooking Network* in less than five."

"*He* got a cooking show," Mom reminded me.

"Yes, because he's the show pony of the relationship. Having an ego the size of Jupiter is Weasel's job."

"Whose job?"

"Derek, Mom."

"Oh, honey, don't call him that. He's still the children's father."

"Would Dickwad or Fuckface be better?"

"See? You're angry. Sylvie's cottage can take the edge off."

I pinched the bridge of my nose. "Of course, I'm angry. Did you forget that he humiliated me, not the other way around? The only reason I didn't get as much airtime on the show was because I was hard at work behind the scenes. I was the driving force in the background, the one keeping the restaurant running while he got all the credit. He owes his celebrity status to me."

"You don't think I know that?"

I swirled my wine as I seethed.

"You don't think I know how hard you worked, day and night, while raising kids and being a wife? Oh, Lily, we may not agree on everything, but honey, I know the daughter I raised. I have never known a more ambitious little girl in all my life!"

Tears welled up in my eyes.

"I don't care who's right or who's wrong, whose fault it is, or anything. I only care about you. I know you're not crazy, but I also recognize someone who needs a break when I see one."

I ran my thumb along my lashes. "Well, you could sound like you're on my side more often."

"I am on your side. Why else would I have asked Aunt Sylvie if it'd be okay? She hasn't set foot in her house in thirteen years, and she's not getting out of her facility anytime soon. We both know she never will, darling." Mom's voice was starting to sound strained. "Honestly, she would be delighted for one of us to use it again."

Maybe my mother really was on my side.

Maybe she always had been.

Still, the Keys were too far; there was too much to do. I had to fight Weasel's settlement agreement or accept it and start looking for new restaurant space in a cheaper part of town. My savings, after Weasel was done with me, would only carry me for three months. Leaving NYC wouldn't solve my problems.

"I'm not that person, Mom." I fought back tears.

"Which person, Lily?"

"The kind who runs away." I blotted my eyes with a cloth napkin and pried open the lasagna foil. "The kind who escapes responsibilities because it's easier than dealing with life. That would be Derek."

"Easier than powering through the pain, you mean."

I stared at greasy, bubbling mozzarella. Suddenly, I'd lost my appetite. Was that what I was doing? Powering through pain? Pretending like none of it ever happened? Biting down, moving on? Wasn't that what the world wanted from me? To get over it?

The truth was: a vacation sounded amazing. To do nothing, for once. To lie on the beach, drink mojitos, and forget my life and feelings sounded like a dream, but life wasn't a dream. The last two years had proven that.

"There's another reason," Mom said hesitantly.

"I was wondering when the ulterior motive would show up."

"It's nothing like that. Don't be dramatic. It's just that Aunt Sylvie is considering selling the place. But she has no family to check it out for her. She needs to see what kind of condition it's in, if it's worth selling, keeping, renting, renovating, razing or what. You could report back to her on its condition."

"Why don't you go then? You're her last surviving sister." I almost added *or send Gary*, but my brain had a hard time remembering that my brother died three years ago. In my mind, Gary was still alive somewhere and would've loved to go spend a week fishing in Florida.

I carved out a square of lasagna and plated it. Instead of holding together nicely, it spread out like a disease.

"And leave your father alone?" She snorted. "Lily, please, your father is lucky I'm there to file his toenails. Besides, I can't fly anymore. My sciatic nerve flares up. You know that."

Yeah, I knew. I knew she was making excuses so that I would take a forced leave of absence is what I knew.

"The kids are grown. They're doing their own thing. Think of it as a transition. Now is the perfect time." The sincerity in my mother's voice made me want to curl up in her arms like I was nine again. "And when you're all refreshed, you come home and start searching for a new kitchen space. Huh? What do you say?"

Nothing disgruntled me more than having to agree with my mother. I did need a break. I did need to get out of my head, but I would have preferred to do it with family, not alone like an old hag.

Bowie jumped onto the counter, squinted his one-green, one-blue eyes, and pressed his cold nose into my forehead. I was going on a trip. "I say you're a stubborn woman," I said, scratching Big Bo between the ears.

"Takes one to know one." A smile crept into Mom's voice. "I'll let Aunt Sylvie know you'd be happy to check things out for her."

"I didn't say yes."

"You didn't say no either." She hung up.

I stood at my kitchen island inside my soul-empty home that used to be a showpiece of pride and joy, a haven filled with laughter. Had it all been an illusion? Not the kids, they were real, obviously. So was their love and dedication, and I thanked the universe every day for them.

But my marriage to Weasel? If I thought about it too much, it would drive me insane. Time away would be good, from these walls, these framed photos of family vacations that would never happen again, the wines we'd collected over the years, the pool we'd built together, the furniture we'd shopped for. The damned granite countertop we'd chosen when we designed our home kitchen, the one featured by *Cooking Network Magazine*.

Our marriage had been purely for show—like one of Chase's video game worlds. Getting away was a good idea. Sea and sand. Fresh seafood. Sunsets. A temporary prescription. Sure, why not. Plus, helping out Aunt Sylvie would ease some of the guilt I'd held onto the last couple of years for not visiting her in Tampa.

It was done, then. After dinner, I would search flights and a rental car. *New latitude, new attitude, here I come.*

2

Arriving at Miami International Airport gave me flashbacks of the South Beach Food & Wine Festival. For years, Weasel and I flew down together. For a week, we'd hop from booth to booth of all our *Cooking Network* chef friends, visiting their restaurants in the evening, doing interviews, getting buzzed under the sun, and having a great time. Well, Weasel would get drunk and have fun. I'd worry about *Chelsea Garden Grill* without us there to run it.

Was everything running smoothly? Was our manager, Carmen Figueras, buying the freshest fish from the market in our absence? I knew she was—Carmen was the best we'd ever had—but she was new at the time, and I still worried. Were our sous-chefs keeping everything organized and our servers making sure our customers were happy?

After a while, I started skipping trips and started staying behind to keep an eye on the restaurant, while Weasel went without me. It just seemed that every time we returned, we'd spend more time catching up on work than if one of us had stayed behind to supervise. The kids were teens at that point; I didn't want to leave them alone for a week and risk them throwing parties while we were gone. As usual, I'd held down the fort while Derek had all the fun.

Another mistake.

Yesterday, I'd passed by the restaurant, pulled Carmen aside, and told her I'd be gone for a while. The divorce and all. At first, she couldn't process how the restaurant would ever run without me there.

"Are you going to do the Halloween thing? The restaurant?" she'd whispered in case anyone could hear.

In the past, I'd confided in her that I wanted to open a Halloween-themed restaurant someday. It just sounded like fun, and lots of business owners were opening fun, themed establishments.

"I don't think so. I won't have the money for anything that elaborate. Right now, I'll be lucky if I open a hot dog cart."

Tears had glazed her eyes and she'd given me a long hug. "You're the best boss I've ever had," she'd said. "I'll miss you."

I reassured her she was the absolute best and could totally do this without me, then I nearly told her how she'd become less of a manager and more of a friend to me, except I felt weird saying so, because her boyfriend of the last year was Dade Parker, one of the network's junior execs. I didn't want her to think that was the only reason I'd befriended her, and didn't want her to feel awkward.

After I left, I broke down for the hundredth time that week, questioned whether or not I was doing the right thing by leaving. I still hadn't decided whether or not to fight Weasel for the restaurant or just let it go, but I would have time to think about it in the Keys.

As I drove through Miami, I thought about my mistakes in perfect hindsight. What an idiot I'd been. All that time, Weasel had been taking advantage of my absence and begun attending events with Miss Tinder in tow, probably disguised as an assistant or publicity rep. My obsession with them almost made me stop on the side of the road to Google photos of past festivals, just to see if I could find them together in any of them. Then I remembered—it didn't matter. They were happy, and I was out one husband. Plus, I hadn't come all this way to continue obsessing. One way or another, I'd have to forget.

In the passenger seat next to me, Bowie sat in his carrier, staring at me through the cage door.

Are you kidding me? What is this?

"Sorry, bud. It was either bring you along or leave you with a cat sitter. We'll be there soon." I took the turnpike exit and started the drive south toward the famous island chain.

Once we reached the first bridge of the Upper Keys forty minutes later, I got an elevated view of my home for the next week. In an instant, I knew I'd made the right choice. Wide swaths of ocean blue, lined by long stretches of sandy beach, greeted me. Marinas swelled with bright white fiberglass boats. The Atlantic Ocean to my left and the Gulf to my right glistened like diamonds under the sun, while steel drums played a melody in my head, a stark departure from Manhattan's cacophony of gunmetal gray and glass (its own beauty, to be fair).

I opened the window, as oven-hot June air blasted through the rental car. Bowie lifted his nose and sniffed.

"Yep, that's the salty air. You'll get used to it."

I'd get used to it, too.

The house was between Key Largo and Islamorada, nowhere near Key West, which wasn't for another two and a half hours, according to my maps app. I could and would visit the Southernmost U.S. city another day, now that I was sure to have extra time on my hands.

I searched for a little island called Skeleton Key on Mile Marker 93, sixty-eight miles south of Miami. The last time I'd visited was in my twenties, briefly, when Weasel and I had stayed at Hawk's Cay and I'd made him drive through Skeleton Key in search of Aunt Sylvie's house of my childhood. At the time, road repairs and barricades had prevented us from reaching the neighborhood, so we never got to see the house. It'd been a good thirty years since I'd last visited, then.

I almost missed the sign. Slowing quickly, I pulled off the highway and turned left toward oceanside, as Bowie's carrier slid off the seat, and I caught it with one hand on the wheel.

Immediately, we were on a narrow road flanked by a wild array of coconut palms and bougainvillea bushes, all sprouting between gravel rocks and moss-covered chunks of coquina. Small one-story houses sank behind trees, and mailboxes shaped like dolphins and manatees leaned, flaky and in need of new paint. Parts of the Keys had swanky, shiny mansions by the sea, but some areas were—let's just say—older with "vintage" charm.

Our tires bumped along the cracked, sunbaked road, but after a turn or two down the wrong street (and one 3-point turn involving pulling into the driveway of an old man staring at me from his front porch rocking chair—I waved at him, but he continued to scowl), I finally found the street I was looking for—Key Lime Lane.

"This is it. Paws crossed." The house was less than fifty feet away, according to my app. If, for any reason, it wasn't habitable, we could always turn right back around and check into the nearest motel.

Finally, we reached 111 Key Lime Lane, and I noted the time. "Ha, 11:11 AM. Cool, huh?"

Bowie cared not about the address-time synchronicity. Bowie only wanted to pee.

I parked and turned off the engine, pulling Bowie's carrier out the driver's side door. As my sneakers crunched on quartz gravel sprouting with weeds, we stopped at a black iron gate rusted by eighty years' worth of island rains. The two-story house I remembered peeked back at us through an explosion of weeds and flimsy beach grass.

Not gonna lie, it'd seen better days.

The quaint Victorian was yellow—or used to be—though most of the paint had faded and flaked, exposing raw driftwood paneling and probably a host of termites. It sat on a half-level crawl space as many Keys homes did, in the event of flooding, and was paneled with lattice screens that drooped and sagged like drunken barflies. If I squinted hard enough, it might have been a pretty dollhouse with porch railing spindles, wooden shutters, and tightly angled rooftop, but if I looked at it with eyes wide open, it was just a dilapidated old house. To think I used to envision this place as mine when I was a child.

"Okay," I sighed. "Let's see what we find."

From his carrier, Bowie hissed. Maybe bringing the big, white beast wasn't such a good idea.

"I know, buddy."

Reaching over the waist-level gate, I undid the latch and pushed it open. "Just an old house. No biggie," I murmured.

I took the porch steps slowly, one solid foot at a time, just in case. Surprisingly, the steps held, as did the porch, though the planks were littered with leaves and dried palm fronds. The front windowpanes, dusty and dark, looked like they hadn't had sunlight shining through them in a while, and the door couldn't have been opened since 2008.

"The frog," I said, remembering my mother's instructions to look for a ceramic frog on the porch containing the house key. Setting Bowie down, I glanced around and spotted the dusty amphibian holding a fishing rod underneath an array of palmetto plants.

I lifted the little guy but didn't see the key underneath, so I searched the surroundings. Maybe it'd been knocked from its hiding spot? When I didn't find it in the bushes either, I walked back to the driveway to see if perhaps it was inside the wrought iron mailbox, which it was not. Bowie meowed nervously from the porch.

"I'm not leaving you, Bo."

I crunched through the gravel and up the steps, ready to check the front door, thinking maybe it was already unlocked—when suddenly, it popped out of its frame and creaked open, pushing the squeaky screen door with it. Ocean currents snaked out, wrapping warm tendrils around me.

"Not creepy at all." I stared into the musty house.

Bowie meowed. *Turn around, human. Take me home at once.*

"No, this is fine. This is good," I said. "You'll see. We're going to eat all the seafood, catch all the fish, drink all the rumrunners down at the local bar. It's fine, totally fine."

An adventure! An island adventure! One day, in the far-off future, I'd laugh about the creepy door creaking open all by itself. Not today. But, one day.

"Hello?" I stepped into the surprisingly cool foyer. In the back of the house, through the living room, I spotted an open window where the breeze was filtering through.

The dining room set was made of rattan, had a circular glass top, four chairs, and faded pink and blue cushion covers with a palm pattern I remembered from long ago. Same with the living room couches, except those were torn along the seams, exposing yellowed foam cushions. Dusty fish art hung on the walls, as well as framed posters of island art begging to be reprinted in vibrant new colors or tossed out completely, for that matter. It wasn't a terrible interior. It just needed major updating.

A lonely, sad time capsule.

I unlatched Bowie's carrier and let the old boy out. He hesitated at first, preferring to sit in the cage than set foot in the house. I went to the car to get the kitty litter and box I'd bought on the way down, set it up, then went room to room, checking everything out. There was power and the fridge felt cool inside, though empty except for a glass bottle of moldy green ketchup. In the pantry were a few cans of beans and a box of bowtie pasta that had darkened and dried beyond recognition. In the oven were two pans and a scratched, glass pie plate.

I floated through the living room across old pine floorboards and stood at the open window. Aunt Sylvie had added a back porch since I'd last visited, along with a mosaic bistro table and two rattan chairs sporting cobwebs that blew in the breeze. If the house felt old and decrepit, that all melted away the moment I took in the view of gorgeous blue-green waters stretching for miles in three directions.

That had to be worth something, right?

I'd have to look into property value of the neighborhood, do a little research for Aunt Sylvie, but I was pretty certain even a ramshackle cottage in an old part of the Keys would fetch a hearty asking price.

But damn, the place hadn't aged well.

Memories of good times as a child came to me, like the time I woke up early in the morning before my parents and brother, and saw my aunt dancing on the beach, spinning while holding a shawl. In her gauzy shift and sunhat, she opened her arms to the ocean like a child to her mother. Her beautiful smile had enraptured me, probably because I'd never seen a woman having fun by herself that way before. In my mind's eye, I could still see Aunt Sylvie walking down the beach, but the memory faded, and the sullied conditions remained.

Wasn't like I'd come for the house anyway, I told myself. I was here for the distance from Weasel. Besides, if Aunt Sylvie let me, maybe I'd paint walls, buy her a few new pieces of furniture, put fresh accents on the walls. I may have been a chef by trade, but we creatives were good at other things, too, and I'd always had a thing for interior design. I could get this place modernized in no time.

Bowie had crawled out of the carrier, hung low to the ground, sniffing and hissing at his new surroundings.

I let my arms down with a slap. "Well, we're here."

We'd made our way down the eastern seaboard from New York City to Skeleton Key, Florida. Here I was—to rest, take a break, "get away," as they say. Reset my life. Rethink my goals. Figure out what was best for me.

I should've felt invigorated.

At least a bit relieved.

But instead, a deep reservoir of sadness bubbled up from my chest, like my soul coming up for air. How did I end up here? Alone without my family. *Sorry, Bowie, no offense.* This wasn't how my life was supposed to go.

WITCH OF KEY LIME LANE

I opened the back porch door, plopped into a cobweb-covered chair, and bawled.

3

After an hour of pity-partying, I headed upstairs to finish my tour. The three bedrooms were just as outdated, and the room my brother and I used to sleep in as kids felt lonely and was cramped with boxes. Seeing all the outdated furniture, I recalled a trip where we'd found a hand-carved Ouija board of my aunt's, and Gary and I ran from the room, shriek-laughing our heads off when the planchette had started to spell A-N-M...

My mother had found out and we could hear her giving my aunt "strong words" about it downstairs. We stopped coming down every summer after that.

"Good times, Gary. Good times," I whispered.

My aunt's bedroom was untouched by time. Her dark wood dresser with the carved moons and suns still sat in the same spot, and the same handmade quilt with the shells and birds I remembered from childhood still covered the four-poster bed. Dirty beige carpeting covered the floors and needed vacuuming.

My to-do list grew longer. I hadn't intended on spending money on this place, but Aunt Sylvie let me stay for free—least I could do was help clean up. Even if she ended up selling, new décor would cheer the place up *for me*.

I'd head into town first thing in the morning to grab a few items.

But first, unpack.

When I headed out to bring my bags in from the car, I noticed four other houses on Key Lime Lane, two on either side facing each other, showing signs of life with colorful lawn decorations, while the other two had boarded-up hurricane shutters, no cars, and weeds that needed trimming. Probably rentals or homes belonging to winter snowbirds.

I dropped everything in the foyer and began setting up Bowie's food and water dish, when I heard a low growl. I turned to find my big beast staring up the rickety old stairs, the carpeted ones I'd just come down.

"What is it?"

Bo's belly pressed against the floor, eyes hinged at the top of the stairs. I followed his gaze but didn't see anything. "It's the settling. You're not used to a beach house." Moving past him, I patted his head which only made him growl harder. "Hey. Be nice, or you don't get the good stuff."

His growling deepened. Maybe a cat sitter would've been better. Now I felt bad for forcing old Bo on my so-called adventure.

As he watched, a light glinted out of one of the upstairs bedrooms. The moment I snapped my sight on it, it disappeared. I laughed it off. There was a lot we weren't familiar with.

I brushed past Bowie and took the stairs two at a time, determined to find the source of the reflection agitating him. The third bedroom faced west, above the front porch, and was empty, except for a few boxes containing clothes, crystals, candles, and journals. In Sylvie's room, however, her window faced the ocean, where I caught sight of a sailboat passing near the shore, its sails reflecting the bright rays of the noon-time sun directly above us, metal loops and boat parts jangling, reflecting light.

"See, silly? It's just a boat—"

I nearly swallowed my tongue when I turned and spotted another cat, not Bowie, standing at the bedroom door.

"Holy hairballs." I pressed a hand to my chest. "Who…who are you?"

The scruffy, dark pewter cat regarded me quietly with big, golden eyes, then looked over its shoulder down the stairwell, at Bowie probably, who was still growling all the way downstairs. It held a curious, protective expression, as though wondering what I was doing here, but it didn't seem afraid in the least.

I hadn't noticed any cat dishes in the house or on the porch, but it was possible the door had popped open again, letting in a neighborhood stray. I would've crouched to try and earn its trust, but the truth was, I didn't want another animal getting comfortable in the same space Bowie would be staying. That was all I needed—cats fighting over territory.

"Alright, nothing to see here. Shoo, go away. Go," I urged the kitty to go back the way it'd come. But didn't the front door have a creaky screen? How had it gotten past that and upstairs without me seeing, or hearing, it?

Bowie, watching the cat come bounding down the stairs, sprinted into the living room, still hissing. Eventually, I'd let him outside. The dark gray cat skittered out the front door, squeaking open the screen, and I was just about to reach forward to close both when I heard a voice on the porch.

"Hello? Lily?"

I pushed open the doors, curious to see who knew my name. An older woman approached the door holding a casserole dish. Her hair was brown streaked with gray, shoulder-length, and a little thin. She wore biker shorts, a pink tank top, leather flip-flops, and had weathered, narrow shoulders.

"Yes, hello?" I peeked my head out.

Bright green eyes smudged with black eyeliner looked at me. "I see you found your way in. Was the door open when you arrived? I gotta get that fixed for Sylvie."

"I'm sorry, I didn't catch your name."

"Oh, I'm Jeanine. I thought maybe you'd remember me from when you were little. I was older than you but not *that* much older than you." When she laughed, it sounded like coarse sandpaper.

"Vaguely?"

If she was, say ten years older than me, she would've been about twenty or so when I was last here. People changed. Especially those who lived under the sun. Her face and arms were heavily wrinkled and tanned. Me, I looked like I'd stepped off an all-vanilla ice cream truck.

I cocked my head. "Did you know I was arriving today, or…"

"We received word. I try to keep in touch with Sylvie, but it's been a while. I also try to keep an eye on her house for her, though I could do better."

"Oh. Thank you. Should I have come to you for the key? I was told to look under…" I didn't mention the frog, in case she wasn't supposed to know about that. I wasn't sure how well my aunt knew Jeanine.

"The frog?" she said. "Yes, should be there."

I stepped onto the porch. "It's not. I checked." I lifted the figurine to show her what I meant, but holy snowballs, there it was. The whole time. I lifted the missing key and placed it in my pocket.

"Did you…just put that there?" I asked.

"Nope. I got my own copy. Not that I ever use it. It's just for emergencies."

I must have been going crazy after all, like my mother said. Maybe Jeanine had borrowed it and put it back? "Huh. That's weird."

The woman laughed and let herself in. "You'll be saying that a lot around here."

"Meaning?"

"This house can be a little strange." She set the casserole dish down on the kitchen counter. "It has its idiosyncrasies."

I wasn't sure what she meant by that and wasn't about to ask. I was feeling the tireds from traveling, so regardless of the answer, I wasn't getting spooked away.

"Thank you so much. What is it?" I peeked under the dish's foil.

"Peach cobbler. Homemade," she said proudly.

"Ooo, yum. I'm always up for homemade dessert." *Chelsea Garden Grill* catered to a trendier clientele. Our desserts were lighter fare, so I missed a good homestyle cobbler.

"I figured. I was nervous making it, being it was for Lily Blanchett and all."

Ah, so she knew me. Also, hearing Derek's last name attached to mine had started to make me cringe.

"But now that I think about it," she said, "I should've made you lunch. How dumb of me, making this when you're probably starving."

"No, this is great. I'm fine. I ate on the road." I patted my stomach. Not true—I was starving so hard, I would gobble up the cobbler the moment she left. "I'd offer you something, but I haven't bought groceries yet."

"That's okay. Just wanted to make sure you knew I was here if you needed anything. That's our house right there, the green one with all the crystals hanging off the eaves."

Glancing through the porch, I indeed spotted all the crystals, and dreamcatchers, and rainbow mobiles, and unicorn ornaments, and stone cherubs, and colorful gazing balls in every color of the chakra.

"Wow."

"Like a happy hippie exploded, am I right?" Jeanine chuckled.

She said it, not me. "I…I love it."

"That's Heloise for you." She shook her head. "That girl could open up her own crystal shop, I tell you."

"Or a portal to another dimension," I snorted.

I never knew how someone would take my jokes. Most of the time, I kept comments inside, but something about Jeanine felt easygoing. I was right. She broke into a hearty laugh. "Wait 'til she hears that one."

"Oh, no, please don't…"

"Did Sylvie tell you about the cruise line?"

"Cruise line?"

"Atlantis Cruise Line. They called her. They've called all of us, those bastards. Going on two years now. Think they can just buy us out, like we're fresh lobster at the market or something."

"I'm not sure what you mean."

"The cruise lines all got these 'private islands.'" She used air quotes and changed her voice to sarcasm mode. "It's a thing. Weekend cruises from Port of Miami don't make it out far enough to the Caribbean, you know, 'cause they don't got time. They have to land somewhere so guests can feel like they're on a port of call. So, they buy small islands, add a water park, a private beach, a few conch shells, a tiki grill, then passengers feel like they've got a resort island all to themselves."

She was so passionately hating this private island idea that she'd worked herself into a cough tizzy. I suspected years of smoking.

"I see. So, my aunt got a call from them?"

She nodded, holding up her finger while she hacked up a lung. "We all have. They want to buy us out. But we won't let them. Skeleton Key's got its history. All these houses, even the ones without anyone living inside of 'em, have all got their history."

"What are they offering, if you don't mind my asking?"

"About a million each island homeowner. Beachfront gets more, obviously. Plus, help getting relocated to new digs."

Now it was my turn to hack up a lung. "A million dollars? But that's great for the islands, isn't it? I thought they were giving you a crap deal, you sounded so upset by it."

"It's probably worth more than that, but most of us don't want the money. Listen. You're from the big city. Someone gives you a million buckaroos, you move from one condo to another. Big deal, right? But what's a million coconuts to families who've lived in this neighborhood their whole lives? There's no beachfront property left in any of the Keys to move to. It's all occupied. This property's more valuable than that."

"That's why they're offering as much as they are."

"But no one wants to move, Pulitzer."

"It's Lily."

"Sorry, my brain said Lily, but my mouth said Pulitzer. Had a great-aunt who worked for Lily Pulitzer back in the day. Had a room in her house filled with fabric scraps, all from Lily's factory. Made us pajamas with her famous designs. Your name reminds me of that."

I considered renaming Jeanine, too—Queen of Tangents. "So, about the cruise line…" I brought us back to the topic.

"That's why your aunt needed someone to come down. To check out the house and let her know if it was worth selling or not. She hasn't been here in thirteen years. Might've forgotten how much she loves it, living up there in Tampa."

"She's quite deteriorated, from what my mother tells me. Her mind isn't what it used to be."

Jeanine's shoulders sagged. "A real shame. Now don't go thinking I only brought you the peach cobbler to try to dissuade you from advising old Sylvie to sell, 'cause I know the house ain't in great shape, and I'm not one for telling folks what to do or not do with their property…"

"That's very kind of you."

"But, just so you know, if all of us say no, it sends a definite message to the company. On the other hand, if even one of us says yes, the cruise line will never leave us alone. They've been bothering us for years."

"Maybe they'll offer more at that point."

Was it just me, or was this a fantastic situation to be in that Jeanine was painting out to be tragic? My aunt stood to make several million dollars from this little shack she'd probably bought for five bucks at a garage sale.

Jeanine looked stricken, like city slickers just didn't get it.

"I understand," I said. "It's not about the money."

Residents loved their island more than oodles of cash. I wasn't about to tell my elderly aunt what to do with her house, but I wasn't going to lie to her either. When she asked how things were going, I would tell her the truth—the house was in disrepair and needed updating if she planned to rent it out. Even to sell it.

"I'll get out of your hair now. I know you're tired. Just wanted to say hello." Jeanine made her way out the door.

"Thanks. I'll be happy to come over tomorrow so we can talk about it some more. Maybe I can meet Heloise?"

"Sure thing." She turned around. "Oh, and if you see a dark gray cat around here, don't mind her. That's just Luna."

"Is she yours? She was just here. You must've seen her when you arrived. Ran right past you. Seemed like a sweetie."

"Sure. For a ghost cat." Jeanine laughed and tapped the screen door on her way out. "Enjoy the cobbler."

4

I watched Jeanine cross the yard, waving to the other neighbor across the street, a handsome younger dude who paused to look at me while carrying bags of groceries. I gave him a half wave then closed the door.

Haha, funny island lady. As if ghosts were real, much less ghost *cats*. Had Luna been a ghost cat, she would've disappeared through a wall, not scampered out the front door, like a real, live, *actual* cat.

I laughed to myself. Even my logistics made no sense.

Had she said it to scare me? Maybe she was irked by my comments about selling. At least I knew what the neighbors were hoping—that I'd convince Aunt Sylvie to keep the house. I understood where Jeanine was coming from. Some things were more valuable than cash. My restaurant was worth way more to me than any money. It was my life, all the more reason I was devastated to leave it behind.

But in certain situations, selling was the easier thing to do, and I couldn't fathom Aunt Sylvie, who required her meals be fed to her, who colored coloring book pages as a brain-stimulating activity, would want to deal with renters for a property she was no longer fit to maintain. I wouldn't worry about it for now.

Too tired for grocery shopping, I took the peach cobbler, sat on a couch with a fork, and ate my first meal in Skeleton Key. It shouldn't classify as late lunch or dinner, but no one was around to judge. Besides, the cobbler was good. Really good. Tomorrow, I'd hit the market, pick up delicious local ingredients, and make an actual meal.

For today, I'd shove the peach cobbler down my throat and call it a night.

I woke up the next morning with heavy period pains, but without the period. My entire life, periods had been regular—every twenty-nine days—but the last two years, I'd had the pleasure of getting them closer together, every three weeks, and unpleasantly heavy. So heavy, in fact, I'd have to use multiple pads or tampons every hour. Sometimes I just sat in the tub to drain. Not feeling like my old self sucked. I caught myself saying things like, "I used to be" or "that never happened before" when talking with my mom.

Oh? You don't like getting older?

Join the club, Lily.

My mother rarely sympathized with the pains of life, as if fearful that any amount of empathy would soften me. As a result, I learned to keep complaints inside, much like my feelings. Softness was not appreciated in this world, not when I was growing up and making my career. If I wanted to get anywhere, I'd have to be tough. Show grit, determination, work ethic, and all that. Like it got me anywhere? I lost my husband anyway.

Yes, I knew it wasn't my fault. Weasel's departure was more about him revealing his true colors than about me. Cognitively, I knew that. But I couldn't help but wonder...if I hadn't been so tough, so determined, so ethical, a workaholic, if I'd been softer, sexier, more eager to follow him around in his travels, rather than insist I manage the restaurant, would he have stayed?

"No, Lily. Shut the hell up," I muttered, rolling out of bed. I wouldn't go down this road again.

I was tired of reflecting, regretting, and reanalyzing all my actions. I did the best I could with the tools I had, with the information and knowledge I possessed at the time. Nothing would have stopped Weasel from finding Miss Tinder and starting a family behind my back. He was just a selfish asshole that way.

As I brushed my teeth and got dressed, I heard the soft ringing of a bell outside. I wiped my mouth on a threadbare towel and headed downstairs with Bowie stampeding after me, as though I would eat his cat food before him. Cracking open a can of meaty shreds, I dumped half the can into his bowl and headed to the back porch.

When I stepped onto the veranda, I sucked in a gasp. The view of the ocean for miles and miles, crowned by pink and yellow cumulus clouds, was glorious. Seagulls cawed along the shore, waves lapped against seaweed strewn sands, and a salty bite was in the air. I couldn't stand here and watch it. I needed to go down and feel it.

I went out barefoot. Ten feet out from the back porch, I plopped onto the sand, remembering when I'd done the same as a child, carrying a plastic blue bucket for making sandcastles. Gary and I had worked so hard to create a complex castle with four towers and a moat, only for some little turd to come careening through, knocking everything down, then laughing at us. Little shit.

Fast forward to forty-five-year-old me.

Same place, same view. Different life experiences. I felt like a crone compared to the child I used to be, when nothing mattered, and the world was my playground.

The little bell dinged again. Shielding my eyes, I looked down the shoreline toward Miami, as rain clouds built up in the north. The sound was coming from the south. I crawled on my butt out further, toes squishing into the hot sand, until waves crept up and kissed them, then retreated back, little bubbles popping like a giggling child.

A man on a small boat, more like a dinghy, was moving along at a slow clip, ringing his bell, and whistling a sailor tune. He spotted me and waved. A little self-conscious that I was the only one on the beach, I waved back sheepishly. Was it customary to come out when a boat man came ringing his bell? I had no clue about island culture.

From fifty yards away, he looked to be in his sixties, gray hair, wearing a baseball hat, tanned, biggish belly. Noticing also that he sat on a large, white cooler, as he navigated the rudder, I realized he was probably a vendor of some kind, an ice cream man of the sea.

"Ahoy!" he called.

That made me laugh. People really said ahoy? I'd only heard that phrase in picture books about pirates and on packages of chocolate chip cookies. I waited with bated breath as he approached.

"Jumbo shrimp, lobster, miss? I also got some conch for your fritters and key limes. Dolphin, too?" He pried open his cooler. From this short distance, I saw his baseball hat said *Get Leid* with Hawaiian flowers for a border.

"Dolphin?" Horrified, I craned my neck to look into the cooler, as he pulled up a nice, fresh mahi-mahi. "Ah, dolphin fish. Got it." Nobody ate dolphins, the mammals, around here.

He put the fish down and pulled up an equally large blue and yellow one. "Also caught some yellowtail this morning. Plenty of those. Hey, you're new. I haven't seen you around."

"You don't miss a thing." I laughed.

"Rented the house?" He gestured to my aunt's cottage behind me.

"No, it's my aunt's."

His twinkling blue eyes darkened in the morning sun, as he glanced at the house, lost in thought. "Ah. Miss Sylvie. Haven't seen her in a while. Give her my best."

"She's not doing well, but I will."

The man dipped his head. "Sorry to hear that." He pulled the boat closer to shore. Then, jumping out of the water, he wedged the hull into the sand. "Tell her Salty Sid says hello. She'll know who you're talking about." He said it with bittersweetness, like perhaps he knew my aunt in some special capacity outside of fish vending.

"Will do. I'd love yellowtail and mahi, but it's just me, and I wouldn't want to freeze the rest. Would you be okay cutting a piece of each for me? I'll understand if you prefer to sell the whole fish."

"I can do that, but you can also make a whole fish and invite your neighbors. Jeanine, Heloise, and Captain Jax would be happy to come over and partake, 'specially with the way you cook." He winked again.

He knew who I was. Guess Aunt Sylvie was proud of me. But had he seen my divorce drama on TV? My classy bonfire on the sidewalk? Inquiring minds wanted to know.

"You know what? I'll take a whole yellowtail, but half a mahi if you're okay with it. I'll also take a bag of shrimp and key limes would be great."

Salty Sid's cheeks unleashed a bright, sunny smile. I'd just made his day. "You got it, Miss Blanchett."

Autumn, I almost said, but I hadn't used my maiden name in ages, and the kids' last name was still Blanchett.

"Just Lily is fine. So, umm... Does everyone know I'm here?"

"We had an idea you'd be coming down," Salty Sid said, sharpening his blade.

"And um, do people know the circumstances surrounding...why I came down alone?"

"You mean, because your ex-husband didn't know a good thing when he had it, so he went and found himself a floozy on Twitter—"

"Tinder, actually."

"Made mini-mes with the floozy, so you rightfully set his shit on fire in front of the house you shared together as a torchlight and warning to all who mess with you? Yeah, they know." He jabbed his knife into the fish's belly and ripped it open from head to tail.

I swallowed. "Oh, good, you have all the details."

"Don't worry, Miss Lily, nobody will ever judge you for what you did. I'd have done the same. Losers like your husband make other men like us look bad. I have no qualms in saying so, if you catch my drift." He propped one foot up against the side of his boat and started scraping off fish scales.

"I...I catch it."

"I was just surprised is all. It's usually men from my generation—and I'm what? Sixty-five—pulling tone-deaf moves like that, but men your age usually communicate more, respect their partners, share in daddy duty, woke stuff like that."

"Actually, he was fine at daddy duty. But you're right, the respect part needed work." Why was I discussing Weasel to a stranger in a baseball cap that said *Get Leid*?

"Don't defend him, Miss Lily." Salty Sid pointed the end of the knife at me. Then, he jabbed it back into the poor fish and started filleting it like a sushi master. Between his life advice and knife-wielding skills, Salty Sid needed his own TV show. "He hurt you," he said with earnest concern and a thin-lipped grimace. "He humiliated you. He lied to you and your kids. None of you deserved that. None of you."

Wow—Salty Sid for the win.

Unsolicited opinions. But still. Winning.

Words failed me. Even a humble fisherman with a rusted dinghy knew I wasn't at fault for what befell my life.

He shook his head. "Ah, there I go again, running my mouth where I have no business."

"No, it's fine. You've been helpful, actually. I appreciate it. Thank you." Back home, nobody talked about my private life straight to my face. They walked on eggshells around me. Here, a stranger with bloody hands had become my new therapist.

"You sure you want the key limes?" he asked.

"Yes? Why? Shouldn't I want them?"

"Oh, sure. It's just you got a whole slew of them in your side yard there."

"I do?" I looked at the small adjacent plot of land I'd yet to explore.

He washed his hands in the seawater then held out a bag of shrimp, along with the yellowtail, and half fillet of mahi.

"Yep. Your aunt's house used to belong to a distiller long ago. Rumrunning Annie was her name, even though she made the booze, not transported it."

Annie. I was sure Aunt Sylvie had mentioned her at some point.

"She hid rum and whiskey in her house for rumrunners to pick up during Prohibition days, but as a front, she sold key lime pies."

"Oh, wow. I didn't know that. That's really interesting."

"Yep, that's how the street got its name. The trees are still there. Been there for a hundred years. I'll be honest, the whole neighborhood goes in there to take what they need when your aunt is not here. Which is…"

"All the time. I understand. No use in letting perfectly good key limes go to waste, I always say."

"These aren't yours." He pointed to his bag. "Just so we're clear."

"Thanks for clarifying." I laughed. Normally, I'd write guys like Sid off as sketchy, but his honesty was refreshing. "Cash, I take it?"

"Venmo." He held out his phone for me to scan his code. Huh. I hadn't taken Salty Sid for an advanced payment option kind of guy. "Go on back there and grab a bunch of limes. Jeanine can show you how to make a pie, but what am I saying? You know how to make a pie. Jeezy jellyfish, listen to me tell a big-time chef how someone could teach her how to cook." He laughed, closed up his cooler, and cleaned his blade in the water.

"It's quite alright. Even old dogs can learn new tricks, Sid," I said.

Sid gave me a weathered grin. "Miss? You're not old. Trust me. You're just getting started."

5

Heading back with my haul, my toes bumped against something hard in the sand. I kicked some aside to find flat planks of wood underneath. Kicking off more sand, I realized it was an old boardwalk. Not the elevated kind, but more of a walking-biking path, except I couldn't tell where it began or ended. Like so many things on this island, it must've fallen into disuse and needed a healthy dose of refurbishment. I mentally tacked clearing it onto my To-Do List, then paused when something else caught my eye.

Glinting in the sunlight about fifteen feet away was a sphere—a glass ball of swirling blue and green, about the size of a grapefruit, attached to the end of a hemp cord, which wound around a palm tree. The ball was tucked under the cord to keep it from breaking. I wondered what it was for, tapped it with a nail.

Such strange sights, this island had.

Trudging back to the house, I dropped everything off in the kitchen, placing the fish and shrimp in the fridge, attacked the peach cobbler again, then whistled for Bowie. He came running downstairs, still low to the ground, still hissing and growling in mistrust of the universe.

"Hey, bud, want to check out the garden?" I unlatched the side door, feeling the wood, swollen with humidity, stick to the frame. I nudged it with my hip. It swung open, bounced against the side of the house, then bounced back again.

The yard on the south side was a veritable jungle of seagrass, grape leaves, mangroves, and God only knew what else. It was an overgrown mess, surrounded by a shoddy wooden fence of tightly fitted planks, no gaps in between. Cat-safe, and I very much doubted that Bowie would want to leave anyway.

Where would he go—the ocean?

"Alright, come on." Snatching my sunglasses from the counter, I ventured into the yard. Bowie lingered in the doorway, unconvinced.

Since the back of the house was east-facing beachfront property, and the next two homes faced north and south, my aunt had a huge corner yard, marked by stepping stones covered in moss, most of them cracked. Skewed wooden planks marked the edges of garden beds long vanished, now overrun with spiky, wild bougainvillea, coconut palms sprouting from the most random places, which shot into the morning sky. Way in the back was the overgrowth of key lime trees.

Jackpot.

They looked like they'd just started ripening, green but not yellow yet, a few rotting away on the ground. If they were anything like the Persian limes I was familiar with, they'd remain ripe throughout summer and early fall. When I plucked a few, they snapped easily off. I collected about fifteen, enough for one pie and maybe a mojito.

Give thanks to the tree.

I paused.

Who said that?

I dropped several limes, then slumped to the ground to pick them up, as Bowie sniffed his way past me.

Give thanks to the tree?

I didn't disagree. As a chef, I was in the habit of silently thanking fish, chicken, pigs, cows, and other creatures who gave their life for our sustainment. It just seemed like the right thing to do. But I'd never thanked citrus before, and that had not been my voice.

"Who's there?" I waited.

After a few seconds, I laughed. As if someone were going to reply. The voice had been in my head, a version of my own, and nothing more. I headed back to the house to drop off the limes when I heard it again.

I said…thank the tree for the limes.

Whoa.

"Thank you for the limes," I said quickly, goosebumps erupting on my arms. Never mind it was on the hotter side of scorching. Nothing chill inducing about this day.

I didn't want to say it. Or even think it. It would mean giving into ideas I rarely entertained, more put out of my mind as hogwash. Like Jeanine suggested, this house, this area, seemed to have its idiosyncrasies. There was something very…uh…enchanting about Skeleton Key.

When I turned, intent on hurrying back to the house, a face peered out at me from inside the mangroves, peeling, flaked, and melancholy, like a religious statue left to melt in the elements. Its eyes seemed to follow me as I moved.

"Jesus." I dropped all the key limes all over again. What the heck?

Heart in my throat, I inched closer to the face in the bushes until logic kicked in, I caught my breath, and could confirm it was just a stony statue or fountain, buried in the overgrowth. I had to steeple my hands over my nose. "Right, Lily, because a live woman would be hiding in the bushes. Get real."

By this time, Bowie had run back to the side steps, preferring to head indoors, as if he, too, were unsettled by the side yard.

Slowly, I stepped toward the statue, noting its realistic— I would even say exquisite—features. A finely shaped nose, French mouth that reminded me of the Statue of Liberty, cherub-like cheeks, and wavy hair, all carved from stone. Parting the bushes some more, I saw she was a mermaid, a defunct fountain about five and a half feet tall.

"You scared me," I told the statue, delving deeper into the bushes. I smoothed my fingertips over her scales. She'd once been painted in vibrant colors. Now she looked mottled with disease. Like the wooden boardwalk or bike path, she awaited rescue from Nature reclaiming her earth.

How cool would it be to restore her?

Another item for my To-Do List.

In fact, this whole garden could be gorgeous again, I thought, but wasn't sure I could work on it in the short time I'd be here. Still, a temporary corner for cooking herbs wouldn't be a bad idea.

As I pulled back to begin collecting the fallen key limes again, the mermaid receded into the shadows, and I took a deep breath to settle myself. What a morning. In just a short time, I'd found a covered boardwalk, a strange glass ornament, a realistic mermaid statue, and heard a strange voice in my head. I had to remind myself that I wasn't in familiar surroundings. I was also still dealing with trauma. My brain was coping the best way it could.

Inside, I started an actual To-Do List. Buy groceries, paint the living room, buy shears for trimming foliage, plant herbs, and, if time allowed, try to get the fountain working again. For someone who wouldn't be staying long, that was a lot—but the idea of having things to do kept my mind off all that awaited me at home.

The food market in Islamorada made everything okay again, temporarily. I felt at home navigating aisles, purchasing the best produce, selecting the best wines to pair with meals, inventing symphonies of flavors. I could've stayed two hours, watching an employee make starfruit marmalade, another offer samples of lychee wine, and the butcher cut and package meats with precision. There was a rhythm to the market, to employees moving in harmonious tandem, that made me feel at home.

When I was done shopping, I stopped by a hardware shop, realizing I should've gone there first so as to not leave groceries sitting in a hot car. Things you don't learn until you're in Florida. I chose a couple of pre-made, discounted gallons of light gray indoor paint, the perfect shade to clear my anxious mind, and a few basic garden tools.

Driving back to Skeleton Key meant entering 1970s suburbia with its coquina walls, carports with concrete breeze blocks, rusted vinyl strap patio furniture, and flamingo lawn décor. They definitely hadn't gotten the memo about 21st century clean lines, but it had its own charm. I'd just parked at the house and popped the trunk when I heard a whistle.

Across the street from Jeanine and Heloise, my beefcake neighbor was in his backyard, waving me over. Just to be sure it wasn't someone else he was flagging down, I checked behind me. "Hi?" I shielded my eyes with my hand.

Note to self: buy a hat.

"Wanna see something cool?" the man said.

That lead-in could be the beginning of a horror movie, I was pretty sure, but I didn't want to seem like the uppity New Yorker, so I inched my way toward his property, making sure I wasn't about to walk into an awkward situation.

"Are you talking to me?" I asked.

"Yes. Come quick. Hurry, there's not usually three of them like this."

I glanced at my groceries. They'd spent enough time in the heat, so I'd have to make this quick, but I ambled through his side gate under a large banyan tree into his backyard, which faced a waterway that fed into the ocean. A 20-something-foot fishing boat called *Sea Witch* bobbed slowly in the water.

When I reached my neighbor, he seemed suddenly taller, easily six feet tall, tanned, with arms and legs sinewed from outdoor work. He wore a captain's hat, and he was pouring hose water straight into the canal. His boat glistened with white droplets, making me realize he'd just washed off the sea salt spray.

"Captain Jax, I presume?"

"Jax is fine, but yeah, that's what Sid likes to call me. Hey, check it out." He pointed into the canal.

I peeked over the edge into the brackish murkiness. No. Way. Three floating gray blimps with paddles and whiskers were chugging away at the fresh water pouring out of the hose.

"Isn't that cutest thing you've ever seen?" Captain Jax's smile was delightful, like a little kid discovering a hermit crab in the sand.

After a lifetime of womanhood, I could always tell when a man was using cuteness in nature to attract me, but in Jax's voice, I heard genuine wonder and glee. Besides, he was younger, in his mid-thirties, most likely, and I was positively certain he wasn't interested in me In That Way. Not that I was interested in him either.

"Are those…" I pointed at the creatures.

"Manatees, yep. Sea cows, they're sometimes called, but look at them. What do you notice?" He crouched by the access ladder to reach down and tickle the smallest one on the forehead while he gave one of the larger ones fresh water as well. The biggest of them just floated there.

"There's two big ones and a little one?"

"Yep, that's a bull right there, plus the cow. And that's a baby. A family. When do you ever see that in nature, huh? God, that is the cutest freakin' thing. You'd think I'd get used to this after living here so long, but I never do." He was so into watching the manatees instead of me that I felt safe knowing this wasn't a flirt trap.

I smiled, more amused by his love for nature than the manatees. I pulled out my phone to take a few pics to send the kids. "That's amazing. The things you see in Florida."

"Right? Every day I find something to smile about. Like look, see those herons over there?" He pointed at two white wading birds pecking in the mangroves with their long, curved beaks.

"Yeah?"

"They've been fishing this canal all week, and just today, I caught them working together. I swear they have a system going where one scares the fish in one direction, while the other snatches it up. Like a team. Blows my mind."

"Mine, too." And as a city slicker, I felt bad that I rarely made the time to watch nature as closely as Captain Jax, who set the hose on the edge of the dock and turned to me. His eyes were all moss and mangroves with reddish centers, and his cheeks were bright and shiny, the way you'd expect from someone who spent time under the sun.

"You're staying in Miss Sylvie's house. What's your name again?"

"Lily, her niece. I haven't been here in years."

"Lily, Lily…" He tried the name out a few times. Did my name remind him of a woman he'd once slept with? Because let's face it, Captain Jax had obviously bedded many women.

"I doubt you'd remember me."

"Actually, wait, Sylvie talked about you. You're from New York. You're a chef, right?"

"That would be me, yes." I smiled.

No sudden realizations crossed his face. I wondered if Jax might be the sole person on this island who didn't know about my private life.

"It's been thirty years since I've been here," I added. The moment I said it, I sounded old. I mean, thirty years was probably this man's entire life.

Captain Jax held my gaze with his swampy hazel eyes so long, I had to look away. I felt my cheeks flush. He chuckled, obviously knowing the strange effect he had on me.

"Lily," he said again, savoring my name. For a moment, I wondered what else he was good at savoring.

I nearly slapped myself.

"I was here thirty years ago," he said. "This is my parents' house."

Oh. He lived with his parents, or just visiting? If so, what concern was it to me?

"They're not around anymore," he clarified in a softer tone. "The house is mine now. If you were here thirty years ago, I would've been about eight. You remember a little blond kid, savage as heck, running around wreaking havoc?"

I searched for a child's face in his handsome, obviously grown, manly features. I looked at the manatees before I blushed again and made a fool of myself. "Wait..."

"Did you come here with your family as a kid?" he asked. "You had a brother named Gary?"

My eyes flew open. "You remember my brother?"

"Dude, your brother was so cool. He made this one sandcastle that looked like a real Frankenstein castle. I was so impressed with him."

"Um, we both made sandcastles?" I tucked my tongue into my cheek. "Just so you know, the design was all my idea."

"But the execution was his. I remember. That dude was epic. Tell him I say hello. Tell him you met the kid that ran right through his work and destroyed it."

"Ah, so that was you! And you're proud of it."

"Hey." He shrugged. "What can I say? I was rambunctious and didn't know how to show my appreciation for fine art."

"And now?" I asked.

"Now I appreciate beauty when I see it." He held my gaze a moment before reaching for the hose and turning off the spout. As he coiled up the hose, an odd silence fell between us. He was flirting. With me. Maybe not a lot, maybe not laying it on thick, but that was definitely a line.

"You should know my brother passed away three years ago," I said. Not trying to put a damper on our fun, but I'd made it a point to tell anyone who'd ever known him.

"I'll be damned. I'm so sorry to hear that. The man was a sandcastle legend, my personal hero for a long time."

I smiled. "That would've made him so happy."

See, Gary? You made another impression.

My brother always felt that, compared to me, he hadn't accomplished much in his forty-six years, and I always had to remind him just how much his creative, infectious personality had indeed influenced others.

Captain Jax had no problem watching me in silence, a smile on his face. I swear he could read my mind, a dangerous thing.

I fanned myself. "Anyway, I have groceries in the car. Stuff's gonna melt if I don't get it inside soon. Thanks for showing me the manatees."

What's gonna melt? I hadn't bought any ice cream or frozen goods. The only thing in danger of melting was me. And "get it inside soon?" Why was it that any words spoken around a hot guy sounded like a sexual innuendo?

"Sure, go, go. Maybe I'll see you later at Jeanine's?"

"Oh, I'll probably be cooking for one, but thanks." That sounded pathetic, but it was true.

"You might want to double check with Jeanine and Heloise. I'm pretty sure they're inviting you over for dinner at seven."

"Really? In that case. Will you be there?" I asked, nearly slapping myself again. I sounded way more hopeful than I'd intended.

Jax beamed. I was so losing this battle. "I wasn't invited. Girls thing only, I think. But no worries," he said. "I'll see you around, I'm sure."

6

Let us review:

A sexy island boat captain thought older-Me was a thing of beauty? Either the men here were bullshit artists, or I still had it. I hadn't used "it" in twenty-plus years, but I still had "it." And as someone who believed I wouldn't have to use "it" anymore for the rest of my life, his unexpected flirting scared the crap out of me.

Captain Jax was definitely hot, and butterflies I'd deemed long dead definitely resurrected inside my dead soul whenever he looked at me, but I didn't need a man with high flirt energy at this point in my messed-up life, at forty-five, just getting out of a 23-year marriage, and *wayyy* out of practice, thank you very much.

Or…was that *why* I needed him?

Gah! Stop sending me mixed signals, Universe!

I brought in the groceries, giddier than I had felt in over a year. A note was stuck to my door: *We cordially invite you to dinner at 7. – J&H.* The door was popped open again. Hadn't I locked it before I left? I should've felt threatened. Back home, it would've been cause for alarm, but for some reason, it didn't bother me.

"Sounds good," I muttered. "I'll bring a key lime pie."

I dropped groceries off in the kitchen, then scooped up Bowie. The big beast purred in my arms, turned his pink nose to me, and blasted his cuteness with lazy, squinty eyes. "Oh, someone's been lonely." I danced with him in the kitchen. "Someone needed a hug."

Bowie made no attempt to jump from my arms like he usually did, and I made no attempt to put him down. We both needed that hug.

Once everything was put away, I grabbed the herbs I'd picked up at the market, a shovel, a trowel, and the bag of dirt from the hardware store and headed out to the garden, leaving the door open so Bowie could come outside, if he wanted to. That's when I stopped in my tracks. A wide-brimmed sun hat sat on the steps. I hadn't left that there. I hadn't even bought a hat yet.

Putting everything down, I picked up the hat, examining it for my aunt's initials or anything tell-tale. Nothing. Just a garden hat that had been thoughtful enough to leave itself out for me, so I wouldn't burn my forehead in the blazing sun.

I remembered a postcard I'd seen at the grocery store earlier today with images of oddball things to find at Key West, like ghost hunting tours, graveyards, and wax figures. *Key Weird,* the postcard said. Now I understood firsthand. Don't ask questions. Don't look for a logical explanation. Just "embrace the weird."

"Oo-kay. Thank you, I guess?"

Was it me or did I feel a cool breeze wrap around me just then?

Slipping the hat on, I mapped out an area for my herb garden—a corner between the house and mermaid fountain would do the trick. That way, the herbs would have partial shade in which to grow. This land wasn't lovely topsoil. It was sand, then hard rock, then limestone, then probably more limestone, though I never got past the sand, because my shovel hit a hardness so hard, even Hardness with a capital H would be jealous.

"That's why little grows here beyond what's native, dumbass," I told myself.

Build an herb garden, she said!

It'll be fun, she said!

I could feel my cheeks on fire, not from the sun, but from internal combustion of physical labor. Still, I resisted the urge to take a break or call it quits. Truth was, I hadn't worked out in a few years and could use a good sweat. It was hotter than Hades.

Finally, after an hour, I took a quick break to make ice cold key limeade, adding lots of sugar to cut the tartness and double the ice. When I got back to work, Bowie slunk out to supervise me from a spot under the bougainvillea bush— smart kitty—but I could tell he wasn't interested in my supercool herbal sand pit. He was keeping his eyes peeled for Luna.

I kept thinking back to my moment with Captain Jax. I knew I didn't want to start anything new until I'd put the old to bed, but the little bit of flirting had been good for my soul.

Look, I wasn't older than dirt, per se, but I weren't no spring chicken neither, if you catch my drift. I'd lost my edge. On second thought, I'd never had Edge to begin with. Sure, I'd been in my twenties once, trim and hot and "sexy" by most men's standards, but here's the thing—I never felt sexy back then. I never owned my youth, and that often made me feel like I'd wasted time.

Instead of dating, dressing up, clubbing, or whatever my peers did at that time, I studied and worked hard. I lived with Derek. I gave him the best years of my life. Now that we weren't together, I often wondered how my life would have turned out different if I'd *gone* dancing, *joined* my friends on road trips, *cultivated* lasting relationships with other women. But I'd given Derek everything. As a result, I had nothing.

Just Emily and Chase. And Mom and Dad.

And this shovel. And a hat.

I was a lot like this garden. Filled with potential, but full of weeds and dryness, in massive need of a makeover.

Once I'd planted the basil, sage, rosemary, thyme, parsley, and oregano, I stood, nearly collapsing from the exhaustion, and observed my work. Nice, but still needed something. I headed out to the beach, hoping to find shells but only finding random pieces of coral and coquina, and came back to place them as a border. Well, what do you know? That actually looked cute. Very quaint, very Instagrammable. I took photos from all different angles and posted them.

Time to shower, then on to make a key lime pie.

Taking off the hat, I wiped my brow. "Let's go, Bo. Nap time."

Beautiful. I'm quite impressed.

Again, not my voice.

I turned. Of course, nobody was there.

I wouldn't ask who said that. I wouldn't feel afraid in my own safe haven. I didn't care if ghosts lived here, I was made of flesh and blood, and sorry, not to be prejudiced against spirits, but that gave me more of a right to be here than they did.

I wasn't sure at first, but I love what you've done.

"Uh…thank you?" I said then quickly grabbed the empty limeade glass and headed inside.

Embrace the weird, I reminded myself.

At 7:00, I glanced into my aunt's mirror with the tacky painted shell border. My long brown hair had dried into natural beach waves, and my makeup, though super light, looked fresh. I didn't know if Captain Jax would be there, but it didn't matter, I told myself for the fifth time. I looked nice for *me*. In my yellow sundress, I looked like Island Lily.

Picking up the pie I'd made earlier—a flaky crust, key lime filling, topped with mounds of delicious baked merengue and drizzled with raspberry sauce—I headed out the door. I was pretty darn proud of my dessert and knew it would blow Jeanine and Heloise away. I was about to lock the door when I thought, *why bother?*

The walk to Jeanine and Heloise's house took thirty seconds. I smiled when I wandered into a land of cherub statues, colorful fairy ornaments, twinkling lights, and, blowing in the breeze off the front porch, a rainbow flag. Ah. I hadn't even considered that Jeanine and Heloise might be a couple. Silly Lily.

I knocked. A short, plump woman with big auburn hair, deep brown eyes, darkest brown skin, and a green and blue tie-dye dress smiled at me. "There she is! Hello! Come in, come in. Welcome to our cottage!" Beaded bracelets jangled as she pulled me into a big hug. "I'm Heloise."

"So nice to meet you," I said, precariously balancing the pie with one hand while I accepted her warm assault. The smell of garlicky shrimp and—I was guessing—buttery noodles filled the house. "I love your home. It's so warm and cozy."

"Thank you! I know I go overboard with the boho stuff, but it's totally my vibe."

"It's beautiful. I love it, actually." In fact, stepping into this hippie dreamland made me feel plain and New Yorker about my all gray and wooden house back home. Note to self: add color and more sparklies to my home.

If I still had a home when I got back.

I handed Heloise the pie. At least I had baking skills. "I made this. Hope my key lime pie passes the locals' test," I said with more than an air of confidence.

I was positive her eyes would go wide with delight. Most people reacted that way to anything I ever cooked, but Heloise examined it from all angles. "That's…so interesting!" she exclaimed.

Jeanine popped out of the kitchen. "Hello!" She, too, stared at the confection, as if not knowing what to make of it. "That's quite a pie, Pulitzer. Come on in." She patted my back and led me deeper into the house.

"I took liberties with it." I scratched my head at what I now realized looked more like a gourmet lemon merengue pie than a key lime pie. "It's probably not what you're used to. Fact, now that I think about it, it's ridiculous, isn't it?"

Wow, I completely bastardized the key lime pie. In the Keys, no less. That's what I got for trying to get food snobby with a local favorite.

"Oh, no, honey, it looks delicious. We love different around here! Don't we, babe?"

"Indeed, we do."

Heloise carried the pie to the refrigerator, then guided me into a small dining room, all set up for dinner.

Nice.

On an Indian-inspired red, orange, and gold tablecloth were three settings, complete with gold chargers, colorful batik printed dinnerware, elephant decorations, more dainty lights intertwined with the wine glasses and silverware, and a bevy of mini sunflower arrangements.

Talk about magical.

A glass of fruity-smelling wine appeared in my hand. "Ding! We don't play around here at the fairy garden." Jeanine tapped my chin like I was eight years old then strutted away, laughing that sandpaper laugh, followed by a deep cough.

"No, you don't." I took in the eclectic odds and ends in every corner of the room. "This is really beautiful. You didn't have to go through all this trouble just for me."

Which, they clearly had, as there were only three place settings. Captain Jax wasn't coming after all. Probably for the best.

The two ladies poured themselves wine as well and lifted their glasses in the air. "Here's to Lily!" Heloise toasted. "May she discover love in the islands!"

We clinked glasses. "Oh, I don't know. I think I'm all loved-out for now."

"There's always space for love," Heloise said with a wink. "Especially self-love."

Ah. Yes. She was right about that. And my self-love needed maintenance, too. "Too true," I said.

I sat at the table while my neighbors got dinner ready and made small talk about today's heat and lack of rain lately. I offered to help but there was no way they'd let me lift a hand.

"You've gone through enough, Lily." Heloise raised an eyebrow, as she fluffed up a delicious looking salad inside a wooden bowl.

"Yeah, let us take care of you."

They whirled through the kitchen in tandem, talking about sights to see while I was here, finishing each other's sentences like twin souls.

My eyes almost leaked. Here were two women I don't remember ever meeting before, treating me to a lovely evening of home-cooked food, cozy relaxation, and warm conversation. I felt blessed, and for the first time in a long time, happy.

"I've lived here a long time," Heloise said, "cultivating my hostess skills, but rarely do I get a chance to show it off. In a way, I envy you, having a restaurant and all. You get to share yourself with others every day."

"That's true," I said, sipping my wine. "Although, after a while, it's easy to forget it's a privilege, because if feels like you're working all the time. Restaurant work can be grueling."

"Oh, I get that, too." Heloise set the salad bowl down on the table, as Jeanine set two other bowls down as well. "Especially in the big city, like you. There's gotta be a happy medium somewhere."

"There is," I said. "I would think here in the Keys, there'd be plenty of opportunities to share your talents with eager customers. This all looks delicious."

"Oh, I couldn't," Heloise said.

"Why not?" I asked.

"I was never trained properly in hospitality. I just love homecooked hostessing is all."

"But that love of entertaining is what sets a place apart. We've all been to restaurants where the food is impeccable, but the hominess, the charm, like this one," I said, gesturing to her beautiful table, "is missing, you know?"

"True, true." Heloise took a seat.

Jeanine scraped her chair along the wooden floor. "Welcome to Skeleton Key, Pulitzer!" She held her glass up again, and I didn't even mind that she'd adopted that moniker for me.

We clinked again. "Thank you!"

After a delicious meal of shrimp in garlic sauce over butter noodles, a pecan, strawberry, and feta cheese salad, and two or more glasses of wine each, things started buzzing.

"So, tell us what made you finally come down after thirty years," Jeanine said, her hand reaching for Heloise's for the first time during the evening.

I looked at my batik inspired plate. "It's like I said before, my aunt needed someone to come check on the house for her."

Heloise adopted a melancholy look in her sad eyes. "And oh, how we miss our dear friend, Miss Sylvie. Do tell her that next time you talk to her. She was like our older sister and mentor."

"I will," I said.

"What else?" Heloise asked. I got the sense she wanted to hear about my personal life, and it was the least I could give her after she'd made this delicious evening happen just for me.

"The rest is the usual. You know, woman gives twenty-two years of her life to a man. Woman finds out man has traded her in for a younger model. Woman finds herself dumped with everything she ever worked hard for gone. The end."

"Tale as old as time." Jeanine shook her head.

"Doesn't sound like the end to me," Heloise said, fist propping up her chin. Her eyes reflected the lights, glazed with intrigue and too much Riesling.

"Nope, sounds like a new beginning." Jeanine played with the stem of her wine glass.

"That's what everyone keeps telling me, but then why does it hurt so much?"

"Because—" They both started at once. "You want to take this one?"

"Nah, you take this one," Heloise replied.

Jeanine crossed her arms and looked at me in earnest. "Because change hurts, Pulitzer. Discovering who you really are hurts. But at the end of the change, a new person emerges. Metamorphosis is painful, love. You think we don't know that? We weren't always together."

"You weren't?" I was surprised to hear that. Jeanine and Heloise seemed like the kind of couple that had been together all their lives, had known each other since before they were born. The kind of twin souls you only ever hear about.

Jeanine gestured to Heloise. "She was married before she met me."

"You were?"

Heloise's eyes had a faraway, sad look to them. "Seems like another lifetime ago. Married for five years. We have a son. He lives in Dallas. That was a very difficult time for me, but it was necessary. Whatever your ex did to you, as hurtful as it was, try to remember it had nothing to do with you. You didn't cause it."

"Feels like I did." I sighed. "I could've worked less, paid more attention to him."

"Nah-ah…"

I looked up from my wine fog to find them both shaking their heads at me.

Heloise took my hand. "You listen to me. It wouldn't have mattered. You didn't cause his confusion, or his unhappiness. He needed to go down that path all on his own. You were an innocent bystander. But in many ways, he freed you. You can do whatever you want now."

"Whatever the hell you want," Jeanine agreed. "Go live on the beach!"

"Yeah, go have hot sex with any guy you want!"

"Or any girl!"

"Or both!"

"At the same time." The ladies bumped foreheads and laughed.

I giggled. "But I wanted him. I wanted my husband. I wanted the life he promised me. That's what I signed up for. I don't anymore, but…"

"Listen to me." Jeanine stared down the length of her pointed finger. If she were a high school teacher, she would have terrified me. "You wanted comfort is what you wanted. The familiar. Right?"

"Not sure I know what you mean," I said.

"If the armoire in your bedroom suddenly went missing in the morning, you would miss that, too. Our brains get attached to things. You know deep in your heart that weasel wasn't your soulmate, but you think you miss him, because he's not there anymore. Not because you loved him."

"What did you call him?" My jaw dropped.

"Oh, babe, that was rude," Heloise told Jeanine.

"No, no, no." I laughed. "It's perfect. It's amazing! Did you know I call him Weasel? Did I call him that in front of you the other day?"

"I don't think so. You're shitting me, Pulitzer."

Now my laughter came out in snorts. "I'm dead serious. That's my nickname for him—Weasel."

"This happens to us all the time," Heloise explained, getting up to go to the kitchen. When she walked, her hair bounced like an orange halo.

"What does?"

"We spend an evening with someone, and suddenly we're guessing their passwords and private tidbits," Jeanine said. "It's a witchy thing. Good energy, mixing together at one table. Information gets passed from brain to brain. We're all part of the same network."

I never believed in that sort of stuff before. She probably just heard me say "weasel" at some point. Coincidences happened all the time.

Heloise returned with my pie and three plates. "Anyway, let's try this baby out."

"My abomination." So embarrassing.

"Now, now. We're open to anything." She served everyone a slice, and the ladies tasted and nodded their heads in deep contemplation. "It's...delicious, that's for sure..." Jeanine said.

"But it's not a key lime pie," I ventured to finish her sentence.

She looked up at me. "We'll teach you how to make a proper key lime pie. In fact, should we tell her, babe?"

Heloise giggled like the fae. "We didn't know you were bringing this. We made one for dessert. Shall I bring that one out, too?"

"Yes!" I nearly screamed. "Please trash mine."

"No. We'll have two." From the fridge, Heloise pulled a picture-perfect classic key lime pie complete with graham cracker crumbs along the whipped cream border and a tiny slice of key lime twisted right in the middle. "Lily, key lime pie never has flaky crust. Always, always graham cracker. The filling is key lime juice with four egg yolks and a can of sweetened condensed milk, and the topping is always fresh whipped cream."

"Never merengue," Jeanine added. "Unless you want to. I mean, this is a free country, Pulitzer. Do what you want."

I laughed. "I botched mine then. Luckily, I have you ladies to teach me the local ways."

"Oh, we'll teach you the local ways, alright." Jeanine unfurled an evil smile. "If you're up for it."

7

The more we drank, the more we ventured into Woo Woo Land. Heloise said I needed an energetic cleansing, so we moved to their backyard—gorgeous, by the way; with a big banyan tree, a mosaic bench and lots of rosebushes, impatiens, and hydrangeas. Though we were drunk as skunks, she and Jeanine tried teaching me to meditate. Unfortunately, my mind was a hamster wheel of negative memories, so when Jeanine said to "clear my brain of unwanted thoughts," it was all I could do to keep from crying.

My soul felt consumed with regret, sadness, anger, and everything I was losing—the house, the restaurant, my dreams, my privacy. My self-respect. I barely had any money to battle Derek in court, just enough to live by, and pay the kids' college for three more months, then I had to come up with a solution. Still, I let the ladies wave crystals over me, because they were supposed to remove negative energy, and I needed that.

Besides, for two hours, I felt like I had friends. I'd lost touch with most of mine. Carmen was the closest thing to a friend these days, but even she now belonged to Derek. I'd delved into work life so deeply, I had nothing left to call my own.

For two more nights, we repeated the dinner parties. We dished on life, drank wine, and told stories. I learned that Heloise (whose family had moved there from the Bahamas in the seventies) had faked orgasms for nearly ten years until she finally got the courage to tell her husband. They parted on good terms, but to this day, she still loved him and regretted lying to him. Though, she also said she needed to figure out who she was.

I learned that Jeanine had always known who she was. So well, in fact, that she dated half the drama girls in high school and college. Back in Kansas City, she was everyone's secret lesbian relationship, but never anyone's main squeeze. When she met Heloise, it was on vacation in Islamorada at a metaphysical store. Heloise had given her a Tarot reading and told her she would find her soulmate soon.

They moved in together the same week.

That was twenty years ago.

The ladies and I also made a real key lime pie together, and I learned, not only that locals were particular about their famous dessert, but that tradition was important to them. As more and more folks moved into the island chain from out of town, they'd watched local culture erode over time.

"Most people who live here aren't from here." Heloise stared off toward the beach. "Eventually, we locals will all be gone."

I understood why they resisted selling their homes to Atlantis Cruise Line, but I'd also seen gentrification happen with neighborhoods in New York and knew that eventually, time changed landscapes.

On the third night, we went harder, and soberer, on meditation. The ladies explained how it was less about quieting the mind and more about going within, tuning in with one's highest self. If you did this enough under the moon, sun, and stars, with your bare feet and butt planted on grass or sand, you connected with the universe. Answers to questions you'd always wondered would come to you. Things you always wished for would manifest.

I'd always sworn this was nonsense, but with Heloise and Jeanine explaining things, it felt possible. At first, I couldn't think of anything except Weasel, how angry his settlement agreement proposal made me, how he wanted to take everything I'd worked hard for, how Emily and Chase had to contend with their father being a liar.

At one point, I started crying, until I heard "shh, shh" from Heloise, felt her warm hand slip into mine, after which point I almost fell asleep. Jeanine said my body was begging for rest, that my mind was suffering PTSD, and I shouldn't set any alarms, just naturally wake up when I wanted.

Unfortunately, my ringing phone did that for me.

"Hello." My voice sounded like Jeanine's.

"Hello, Lily, it's Mom."

"I know. I always know it's you. Just for the record."

"Well, you sounded so hoarse, I wasn't sure you'd recognize me."

"It's all the yelling at paparazzi I've been doing."

"Really?"

"No. I'm attempting to joke. Skeleton Key is the chillest island on the planet. What's up?" I sat up and rubbed my eyes.

"Have you had time to assess the property in between all your galivanting?"

"I haven't been *galivanting*. I've been wallowing in my misery. And no, not really. Can I call you back?" I needed to pee and didn't want my mom to hear it, or she'd surely have an opinion on that, too. I hung up.

Once I'd gotten dressed, made coffee, and fed Bowie, I felt I could tackle a phone call with my toughest critic. But first, I pulled all the living room furniture into the center of the room, so I could start painting.

My mother answered on the first ring. "Did you send your man visitor away, so we could talk?"

"What? I don't have a man visitor. I just needed to wake up without an inquisition. Which I'm ready for now, by the way. How detailed a report is Aunt Sylvie expecting? I mean, I have my initial impressions of the house that I can share."

"Fine, let's start with those."

I set the phone to speaker, while I cracked open a can of light gray paint. "The house needs serious updating. The kitchen is old, the stairs are old, the carpet is musty and dirty, the pine floors are worn, the windows are the old jalousie kind..."

"Oh, I know. They're dreadful."

"The garden is overrun with weeds, although I did turn one corner into an herb garden."

"That's my girl, making lemonade out of lemons."

"I've done that, too. So, structurally, I'm not sure. The porch seems rickety in spots, and the A/C probably needs replacing."

"Will it cost a fortune to update?" she asked.

"We're talking a nearly hundred-year-old house that hasn't changed much in that time. Do you want me to get a property inspector out here?"

She sighed. "I don't think it's necessary. I think she'll definitely be selling. Don't know why she hasn't already."

I thought of what it must've been like for Sylvie living here all those years, having the beach to herself, Jeanine and Heloise as neighbors, the nightly fun, Sid... "She must have her reasons, Mom. Let her decide whatever she wants."

I didn't tell her that I was starting to take to the house myself. Or that I was about to paint. I'd rather do it and apologize later than be told not to bother. No matter what, rent or sell, the house would need new paint.

After a moment, as if Mom could read my thoughts, she said, "Lily, between you and me, I'm not sure Aunt Sylvie can make this decision on her own. At times, I have to remind her who I am, who you are…"

I stared out the window at the ocean that Aunt Sylvie would probably never see again. "That bad?"

"Yes. And when the time comes to speak to the cruise line, I'm certain I'll have to be the one handling things. From the sound of it, might be better for Sylvie to take the cash and run rather than put any effort into renting it."

I swallowed a lump in my throat. The thought of Aunt Sylvie wasting away so close to the house she loved without enough agency to make decisions killed me.

"If it comes to that, we'll deal with it. But listen, there's a whale in my backyard right now, looking through the jalousie window, so I have to go."

"Really?"

"No. Whales don't live here. It's a dolphin. They're so needy," I joked.

"Very funny." My mother let loose a small chuckle. "It's nice to hear you smiling again, honey. Talk to you later."

I did have a smile on my face, didn't I? And I had cracked a joke, hadn't I? That was nice.

I got to work removing fish art, faded peach and gray framed posters of shells, and shelves with knick-knacks off the walls. Dusty crystals and beads, shells holding sand and ashes, a stick of half-burned wood. Odd Sylvie things.

I'd only gotten one wall painted when already, it made such a big difference. Funny how a little paint could change the entire energy of a room.

"That looks so, so good," I said.

I reached for the paint can, to add more into the tray, when I heard a voice: *It absolutely does.* I gasped, jerking around and scanning the room. That sounded real. Not in my head, but out in the open. Bowie was asleep in the back window.

"Okay, who is that?" I asked out loud.

No reply.

Above me, the ceiling fan whirred, its chain tinkling against the metal center.

"Why is it when I talk straight to you, you don't answer? Who's here?" I demanded. Heart in my throat. Ready for anything.

After a minute of standing with paint dripping down my arm, I caught something out of the corner of my eye. My breath caught in my throat. "Geez…" I hugged the paint stick to keep from falling.

Luna stood by the stairway. The stealthy gray cat blinked her golden eyes. Call me crazy, but she seemed to be admiring the new wall color.

"Was it you?" I asked. "Are you the one talking to me?" I had to laugh. As if a cat could talk.

Bowie looked up, growled at Luna, and feigned going back to sleep. His wary eye remained on her, but he no longer seemed agitated or scared. It took a week for him to get used to her.

I squatted. "Come here, girl. I won't bite."

Luna gave me happy, squinty eyes but didn't budge. I approached slowly, hoping she'd stay in place until I reached her, so I could demonstrate my trustworthiness, but there was a knock at the door.

I leaned the paint stick against the wall for one second, and when I moved toward the door, Luna was gone. "Seriously?"

Jeanine's comment—*ghost cat*—swam through my mind, even though Luna wasn't filmy or see-through. I could see her entire, solid body.

I opened the door and there stood a very rugged, very ready-to-do-yard work Captain Jax, wearing his captain's hat and holding a long pole with a sharp, curved scythe at the end.

I crossed my arms. "Alas, Death has come for me. I was not ready."

His chuckle could set my shorts on fire. "I was cutting down coconuts at Jeanine's. Want me to make that tangled mess you call a yard unrecognizable?"

"That would be amazing. Thank you!"

He stepped inside. "I used to play back there, you know. As a kid, I'd sneak in. Sylvie would catch me, tell me I didn't need to sneak. I could knock and she'd let me in, as long as she was home."

"Aww." I smiled, remembering Sylvie in her hat, her wraparound, and her deep suntan. It broke my heart that people grew old. "She was probably happy to see you playing in her yard, since she didn't have kids."

"I was always the errand boy between her and my mom. *Take this to Sylvie. Ask Sylvie if she's got any limes. Give this book to Sylvie.* As she got older, kids from other neighborhoods made fun of her. Said she looked like a witch."

"Ugh. Why are kids such assholes?"

"I don't know, but they biked from other parts just to call her that." He closed the door and stood there, looking like a golden Adonis. I diverted my gaze, pretending to be interested in the wall. "She was the coolest lady. Always gave me those stick popsicles."

"I remember!" My memory flew back thirty years to the ice popsicles Aunt Sylvie always gave us when we were building sandcastles. "Oh, man."

"Jeanine, Heloise, my mom, and Sylvie used to hang out on the beach at night. I never knew what they were doing but hearing them laugh late at night while I was supposed to be sleeping was a big part of my childhood."

"And your dad?"

"He didn't care. My dad spent his life watching sports from his La-Z-Boy. I was an outdoor kid into bird-watching, fishing…so I ended up on your aunt's stretch of beach a lot. Anyway, this door is loose." He started fidgeting with the screen.

I smiled sadly, my guilt at an all-time high. I definitely had to visit Aunt Sylvie before I went back to NYC. Seven days had zipped by in a flash. I'd have to check my calendar soon to see whether or not I should extend my stay.

A series of texts came in just then, all from Weasel. Said he'd heard from my lawyer, and there was no way he was sharing *Chelsea Garden Grill*. He was the face of the restaurant, and how would it look to have us both there? I had to be reasonable. I should show a little self-respect. I had to think of my future. I had to think of the kids.

"One second," I said to Jax, then turned around to engage in a text war:

> *I have to be reasonable?*
> *Me? I have to be respectful?*
> *Choice advice coming from you.*
> *Do me a favor and leave*
> *me the hell alone.*

> *Oh that's right you're in Florida*
> *avoiding phone calls from your lawyer*
> *and telling Carmen not to listen to*
> *anything I say.*

> *What??*

> *I've barely spoken to Carmen since*
> *I left. If she's not listening to you,*
> *it's your own damn fault.*
> *It was me she collaborated*
> *with on a daily basis.*
> *You have to earn Carmen's respect.*
> *Guess you still have a lot to learn*
> *in that department.*

"I'll just…get to work." Captain Jax swished by me and poured out the side door to the garden.

*You can't stand the fact that
I'll be running the day-to-day
on this place can you? What
will you do without your
martyrdom?*

*I'm not doing this.
Goodbye.*

Goodbye had become the automatic word we used when we couldn't take another bullet. I threw the phone onto the couch and followed Jax outside.

"Loser." I grabbed the sun hat and slammed it on my head. The mermaid statue stared at me. Would it be insane to say she looked sympathetic?

"I'm not even going to ask," Jax said, clipping branches, making a pile in the middle of the yard. His arms were golden brown from the sun. I'd be lying if I said they didn't look pleasant to the eye.

"Good, it's not worth it." I didn't feel right with him doing all the work, so I grabbed the small shears and trimmed away at smaller branches. "Tell me your story. I can't take my own much longer. You live alone in your parents' house?"

"My house," he clarified.

"Sorry, didn't mean to imply you mooched off your parents." *Good one, Lily.*

"That's alright. They died within a year of each other ten years ago. They were older, had me in their forties, and well, when my father died of a brain aneurysm, my mother followed soon after."

"That's so sad. I'm sorry."

"It's how they would've wanted it. I rented the house out for a while, but when my ex-wife and I split up eight years ago, I came to live here. Brandon used to visit on weekends, but once he turned sixteen, he started staying at his mom's. All his friends are there."

"Where's his mom?"

"Pembroke Pines. About an hour drive."

"Ah. They all go through that 'friends' phase," I offered. "Try not to take it personally. Sorry you don't see him, though."

He nodded, kept trimming the bougainvillea bushes. "He thinks I did something wrong to make his mother not want to be with me anymore. But it's not true."

"That's boys for you, taking their mother's side."

"I did nothing wrong. I was true to her the whole time. I loved her. My biggest crime was that I didn't make enough money."

"Finances were an issue?"

"As a freelance insurance agent? You bet. Once we split, figured I'd do what I always wanted that my ex never agreed to."

"And that is?"

"Charter a boat in the Keys. So, here I am, living the dream." He extended his arms, gesturing to all of paradise.

"Yeah? Business is good? That's great!" Glad to hear someone was doing well!

"Business sucks."

"Oh." My pride deflated.

"If you don't purchase ads with TripAdvisor or you're not on all the tourist directories, people don't find you. I'm sure Jeanine has told you she doesn't want to sell her house, that most residents don't want to, but some of us need the money. I've considered it. I wouldn't have to worry about where my next paycheck will come from. I don't know."

It made sense. Atlantis Cruise Line was offering a fair amount. This could work out for Jax.

"Maybe it's a matter of making yourself more visible," I suggested. "Do you have a website? Or an Instagram page where potential clients can find you?"

"Nah, I'm not good with tech or social media stuff. I always feel awkward self-promoting, like I'm tooting my own horn."

I couldn't believe the sheer potential trimming trees in my yard. This man could get dozens of clients a week if he just tweaked a few business practices. His rugged looks alone could book bachelorette parties galore. I thought of that handsome carpenter on Instagram who posted videos of himself dancing while on the job. The dude had millions of followers.

"You have to make it a lifestyle," I explained. "Instead of begging people to charter a boat from you, you post trendy photos of yourself on the ocean, fishing or whatever. Or a pic of the manatees we saw the other day. People love looking into other people's lives. They'll 'like' your photos, because you're passionate about what you do. They'll 'buy into' your lifestyle."

"I get it, but I'm just not good at it. You're used to it."

Sounded to me like Jax was telling himself a sob story just so he wouldn't have to change. Maybe divorce had been enough change for one lifetime. Some people found change so difficult.

Said the woman who burned her ex's things on the sidewalk. I frowned. I was no one to judge.

"I wasn't always good at it," I said. "I had to learn. Trust me, you can do this. I'll help you build a simple website, a landing page where people can find you, an IG account…"

He gave me an appreciative smile. "You don't have to do that, Lily. You have enough on your plate."

"I'd be happy to—really. Let me finish painting tonight, and I'll help you out. Hey, you said my aunt used to gather with Jeanine and Heloise on the beach back in the day?"

"Yep. The four of them, my mom included, used to have what they called moon parties."

"Moon parties, huh?"

"Yep. I might've bulldozed through your brother's sandcastles, but when it came to those four's shenanigans, I steered respectfully clear. I'm sure if you ask Jeanine about it, she'll fill you in. You might need to get her drunk first." He winked.

"Thanks for the tip."

Meeting under the full moon? Knowing Heloise and Jeanine, there were more "ways" to learn about, and like any good neighbor, I was going to find out.

8

A funny thing happens when you paint an entire room. Suddenly, you have a snowball. Now you have to redecorate that room, change the whole feng shui of the room, buy new décor to go with the new look of the room…

The gray walls came out so utterly fantastic, it looked like a new house, and I kept stepping onto the porch and walking back in repeatedly just to see the effect it would have on me.

Calming.

That evening, I spent an hour sketching what the other rooms might look like in a journal I'd brought along for soul-searching. So much for that. Without knowing what Aunt Sylvie's plans for the house were, there was no point in redecorating everything, but maybe a few new furniture pieces would do my soul good, too.

In the morning, I headed to Marathon, an hour south on Overseas Highway, determined to find basic furniture that looked both modern and classic, not too expensive. Without a certain future, I couldn't overdo the spending. I found one place that specialized in furniture with an island look that wasn't rattan. I knew its dark brown frames with linen cushions would complement the gray and white of the walls.

The store would even deliver it the next day for a small fee, so I left Brian's Island Barn feeling like I could teach a MasterClass at Redecorating. Across the street was a boat rental shack with lots of colorful kayaks in a row and a short line of people renting them. Something told me to go on over there and sign a release form. Since I'd been here, I hadn't done anything sporty.

But you didn't bring your swimsuit.

What if you fall into the water?

What if you drown?

Shut up, brain, always looking for excuses not to have fun. I'd always wanted to kayak, and Florida waterways were the gentlest, stillest waters on the planet. What was the worst that could happen? Mangroves might reach out and scratch me?

I pulled into the Kayak Shack, signed a few forms, and received a life vest and oars. I listened to a bronze, taut, petite goddess wearing a visor (who made me feel older, the longer she talked), as she showed me how to use the oars, maneuver backwards, and call for help if I needed it. Within minutes, she had me climb into the kayak and launched me into the gulf with a flip-flopped foot. Soon I was adrift.

Within minutes, I'd gone from furniture store madness to crossing the bustling highway, to listening to families chatting by the dock, to now complete and utter silence. At first, I took a few obligatory Instagram photos.

Look at me having a great time!

Look at me in my life vest and orange kayak, having fun in the sun!

Woohoo, don't I look independent and adventurous?

Divorce is fun!
I don't need you, Derek Blanchett!
I don't need anyone!

But eventually, I'd drifted far enough from the dock where it was just me, nature, and quietude, all getting reacquainted. Open water felt overwhelming and unnerving, so I paddled toward the mangrove system on the map Miss Bronze Goddess had given me.

There, a few egrets grazed in the shallow root system, peering up curiously as seagrass dangled from their beaks before returning to fishing. Blue crabs scuttled on the roots, as pipefish flitted just below the water's surface. With each dip of the oar, warm water ran back the length of the pole, down my arms, until my seat was soaked.

I didn't care. This was beautiful. And peaceful.

But once again, I was alone.

Too alone.

My therapist once mentioned how I needed to get used to being alone, not because I'd end up that way, but because I should feel comfortable and happy being with myself. She suggested that in all of my forty-five years, I'd never practiced loving myself. She was right. All my life, I'd given my power to the men around me.

I took advantage of the solitude and tried Jeanine and Heloise's meditation techniques. Taking in a deep breath, I closed my eyes and imagined a white light covering me from head to toe. Tried to imagine power radiating through me, filling me with pure potential. When nothing happened, tears burned my eyes.

What would it take to feel good again?

What would it take to forget?

I stopped rowing and drifted, letting the waterway guide me, maze after maze. According to Heloise, I was a powerful woman, filled with mystical crone energy, and I needed to harness that power. So, why did I feel so defeated? Even now, surrounded by such beauty?

Jeanine had said meditation wasn't quieting your brain. It was accessing the real you inside. Well, this was the real me—sitting adrift in a boat, sad, lonely, and angry. The sooner I recognized my shadow side, the sooner I could heal from it.

I entered an open area of beautiful, private homes. Little kids played on the docks and waved at me. I waved back. The sun was becoming a tangerine ball low in the sky.

I needed this kayak.

But then, my phone vibrated, and though I knew I shouldn't look, I did. It was Emily, and when GenZers called, it was usually serious.

"Silly billy! Did you see my pics? You didn't think your mother was capable of rowing a boat by herself, did you?"

"Mom, I'm not calling about the pics."

"Are you okay?" My stomach plummeted.

"Remember how I told you I was spending the weekend with my friends, Nia and her boyfriend, and you said that was fine, and I said cool, I would just stop by the house to pick up a few things?"

"Yeah…" Truth was, I didn't. I was busy downing three glasses of wine with my neighbors.

"Well, I went by. And guess who was there? Dad."

My blood curdled. I stared ahead at open water, at the sun splitting into an array of beautiful citrus colors. "WHAT."

"I asked what he was doing there, and he said he was picking up the 'last of his things.'"

"The last of his things turned into bonfire smoke. I can't believe this." I switched my screen from phone call to text, my fingers ready to go to war.

"Don't you have a restraining order against him?" she asked.

I didn't know she knew about that. "Yes, but I suppose because I'm here…"

Emily was charged up. "So, I told him there was nothing left, and you know what he said? He said actually, there were DVDs there that he wanted to show his kids—his *other* kids, Mom. Can you believe he said that? He said he took the Miyazaki movies that Chase and I used to watch, because his *other kids* wanted to see them. *My* Miyazaki movies, Mom! Is he insane? Those were mine!"

I could hear the tears in her voice and felt the rage building up behind mine. "This is bullshit. He can download those movies any time he wants. He doesn't need to break into the house for them."

"He was snooping, Mom."

"He was there looking for stuff to help his case, go through my desk, steal shit, because he knows I'm out of town, and you're out of town. Lying sack of shit. I'm sorry, that was wrong of me. I know he's your father."

I couldn't keep the fury out of my voice. For so long, I'd tried protecting Derek's honor in front of his kids, but now he'd gone too far.

"But he's being a dick!" Emily cried. "How did he get in if you changed the locks?"

"Honey, he lived in that house for fifteen years. He knows which windows don't seal right. The back French

79

door has never closed right. I'm going to nail him for this. Did you take pics? Of his car in the driveway? Anything?"

"Mom, no. I was so shocked to see him there. I'm at Nia's now."

"Oh, honey. Okay, listen. Go on your trip. Have fun. Don't worry about it again. What he's doing isn't right, but it's not our fault," I echoed what the ladies said to me the other night. "None of this is your fault. We have to just let him go. At some point, we have to move on. I'm sorry, Emily. I love you."

"I love you, too, Mom. I'll send you pics. I just saw yours. That sky is insanely beautiful. Have fun."

"I will, honey. Thank you for calling me."

I hung up. My hands shook like crazy, my tears on the verge of spilling, the wrath in my chest on the verge of detonating. How dare he go inside the house that used to be ours? How dare he break in? Who cared what he needed? Derek really thought he was above everything, didn't he? It was the sneaky way he did everything, the going behind people's backs, the fact that he had re-entered a space I'd worked to make safe again.

Was nothing sacred?

I couldn't even scream in frustration out on this kayak, or people within earshot might think I was in distress. All I could do was sit here, let my chin drop, and allow my tears to silently spill from my soul. Somehow, I needed to get past this. Somehow, I needed to reclaim my life and become that nerve center of crone power Heloise and Jeanine said I was.

After returning the kayak, I drove home determined. Pissed. Ready for change. I parked outside Heloise and Jeanine's house, spotted Luna blinking down at me from the roof, and knocked on the door.

Heloise answered, holding a broom, looking satisfied with herself. "Well, hello, sugar," she drawled. "Figured I'd be seeing you. Felt that rift in the Universe a mile away." She laughed.

"What's a moon party?" I asked. "Whatever it is, I want in."

9

Out in the garden, we sat under the banyan tree where Heloise prepped and offered me a hit of her weed (I hadn't even realized she smoked). Her deep brown eyes filled with concern. "Will this help?"

"Oh, I'm fine. Thanks."

"Are you okay with me…?"

I nodded. I'd never been a smoker myself but had no problem with others doing so.

"Tell me what happened."

"It's Weasel. My daughter called; told me he broke into my house."

"Broke in?" Jeanine joined us and took a seat on the mosaic bench. Now two sets of eyes gazed at me.

"Basically." I explained everything, how Emily was passing through on her way to a weekend gathering when she found her father at our house, how he claimed to be picking up DVDs to show his other children, but Emily called him out.

"She knew it was bullshit," Jeanine said.

"Your daughter's perceptive, Lily."

I nodded. "She told me once, years ago, that 'Dad goes on a lot of business trips, doesn't he?' This was before we knew about his double life. I explained that his job required travel, that he was the face of *Chelsea Garden Grill* and was contracted to appear at events, but I think about her observation all the time."

"She sensed his cheating. She knows he's bullshitting now, too." Heloise took a drag of her blunt.

"She does."

I stared at a tree filled with yellow frangipani. What a beautiful place to be miserable.

"What pisses me off is the sheer invasion. He thinks he's above the rules. He thinks he can do whatever he wants. But that house is mine." My voice shook with anger. "It may have his name on it, but I'm the one living there. He forfeited that house when he left, when he cheated."

"I know that's right," Jeanine said.

"I haven't fought for much in the last year," I confessed. Hearing me say it aloud helped me become more aware of it. "But that's because I wish it would all end, so I've—"

"—given in to everything he wants," Jeanine finished my sentence.

"Yeah, I've been too nice. But that ends now. If I don't fight for the house—for anything—he'll walk all over me," I said.

"Shoot." Heloise sat back and stared at the trees. "Okay, look, I'm not saying you don't have the right to be mad, because you do."

"Hell yeah, you do," Jeanine threw in.

"But I don't think fighting harder is the answer, Lily. Honest to God, what I think you have to do is let all this shit go."

"But he broke into my house." Damn these useless tears. I flung them away in disgust.

"Honey…" Heloise passed the joint to Jeanine and took my hands gently. "It's not really your house anymore. Even if you win the house in your battle, his energy will always be there. His imprint. Do you really want to live in a house that will forever be haunted by your ex?"

"Being dead is not a requirement to haunting someone," Jeanine added in Jeanine's special way. "I get that you're angry—I would be, too—but holding onto anger keeps you trapped."

"Which is what he wants," Heloise added. "And you don't want that."

I looked at them. I knew eventually someone would tell me this. They were right. On one hand, I felt like fighting, but on the other, I would never move on if I did. Somehow, I had to find a future without relying on the past.

"I can't stay there, then." I shrugged. "You're right. He will always be around. The house will forever remind me."

"I'm not saying you should move out right away. Just saying, it's something to think about." Heloise squinted her pretty eyes into the sunset, stood, and tapped a fairy hanging from an ornament. It made a tinkly, musical sound.

I was pissed he'd broken into the house, but there was nothing there to incriminate me, assuming he'd been looking for blackmail. I never hid a damn thing from him in all those years. I let go of the issue…for now.

"So, what's this about moon parties?" I asked.

"Who told you about that? That's top-secret information," Jeanine joked. "Let me guess. Captain Manatee?"

I allowed myself a tiny laugh. "It might've been him. He said my aunt used to do them with you. Whatever it is, I need it. I need this magic in my life."

Jeanine leaned back in her seat. "I don't know, Pulitzer."

"What don't you know?" I didn't even care that the famous fabric designer's name had stuck. I needed a new identity anyway. "Sounds like you don't think I'm ready."

"It's a lot of woo-woo shit."

"I can be into woo-woo shit," I said.

"Can you?" She eyed me sideways. "Are you sure? Because what you've seen so far? This house? This is only the tip of the woo-woo shit iceberg in this house."

Heloise gave her a mildly offended look. "I'm sorry, does my woo-woo *shit* bother you, babe?"

Jeanine reached for her hand. "Never. You know I love it."

Heloise rolled her eyes. "There's a new moon in three days. Time for renewal. When you go home, get yourself a nice glass of wine, a blank sheet of paper, and a pen. Sit down somewhere quiet—the garden, the beach…"

"The toilet," Jeanine said.

I laughed out loud.

Heloise was about to retort, but she turned back to me. "The whole idea is to shed what no longer serves you. You're going to say goodbye. Ask the universe for a clean slate. Purge what no longer belongs in your life."

"Like I said, a toilet." Jeanine took the blunt from Heloise and drew on it. "I mean, isn't that where we put stuff that no longer serves us?"

"You know, in the nastiest possible way, you're right," Heloise sighed. "But for the sake of brainstorming a list, choose somewhere peaceful, Lily."

I looked at Jeanine, expecting the next joke to be cracked. After all, toilets could be a peaceful place, but she kept her grin to herself.

"What do I do then?" I asked.

"You're going to write all the things in your life that you want to let go of."

"That's going to be a mile long," I scoffed.

"And that's fine. Make it as long as you need but focus on the most important ones. Old habits, gone. Lies we tell ourselves, gone," Heloise said.

"Weasel's display of dominance over my life by invading my private space? Gone," I said.

"Exactly. Then, on the new moon, you're going to light a candle and meditate, just like we showed you here. Find a place where you can release the old. You're going to be burning the list. Not your aunt's house—you don't want ashes staying with you. You want it gone, so go somewhere where the energy will leave you. They say crossroads," Heloise said.

"But we wouldn't want you to get hit by traffic," Jeanine said. "A traffic-free location is best."

"A place where water will carry the ashes away, like Jax's canal, for example," Heloise said.

"Wouldn't the ocean work?" I asked.

Heloise shook her head. "Not your backyard. The ebb and flow of the waves will bring your ashes back to you. If you had a boat, I'd say take it out far. Or drive to one of the bridges. You can take one of my small prayer candles. It doesn't have to be fancy."

"She can have Jax take her out on his boat," Jeanine said.

"No, she needs to be alone," Heloise said.

"True. Look, Pulitzer, the point is you're going to be saying goodbye to that shit," Jeanine explained. "Say each item aloud. Say 'I release you from my life. You no longer serve me.' Imagine each stress leaving you. Watch each one ride into the sunset, never to be seen again."

"Yes, then you burn the paper…" Heloise said.

"You can also write each item on separate strips of paper, if it's easier," Jeanine clarified.

My face bobbed back and forth between the two women. Somehow, I imagined magic to be more about wizards and fireballs, but this felt more real. Practical. I preferred it.

"True," Heloise said, "then burn each one, one at a time, as you let it go. It's symbolic. It should feel right. Then, thank the universe and let out a big sigh. Really feel the heaviness around you float away, everything you've been carrying on your shoulders, the guilt, the rage, the sadness…"

"I'm going to lose ten pounds when I'm done," I laughed. "Okay, so that's a moon party?"

"Nope," Heloise said. "That's a new moon ritual. The party comes afterwards. We do them twice—once on the new moon, once on the full moon, to bring good things into existence."

"We do them more than that," Jeanine said. "We don't need much of a reason to party on the beach."

Both ladies looked at each other and cackled.

"I can do this," I said. "You gals are giving me life."

"We'll meet you on the beach behind your house, just like we used to do with Sylvie. It'll be dark. Bring wine," Heloise said, tapping her fingers together.

"Bring your naked body, too…" Jeanine snorted. "Don't worry. We won't look. Nobody cares."

"Wait, what?" My eyes popped open.

"Hey, you said you could handle the woo-woo."

Heloise slapped Jeanine's hand. "Stop. You're freaking her out." She turned back to me. "We'll show you the rest then, okay? The lack of clothes is optional. Symbolic of a clean slate. No more burdens to carry around."

"Wow." I drew in a deep breath. "Thanks, guys."

They looked at me and smiled. "We're glad you asked, Lily," Heloise said.

Jeanine said, "In a way it'll be like having Sylvie here again."

In the distance, I heard the bell of Salty Sid's boat and soon after, the whistling of his sailor-pirate-y tune. "I know what that sound means."

"An old coot is here?" Jeanine said.

"Aww, he's a nice old man." I laughed.

"Let me guess, he told you that all men suck, except for him? He's so humble. Get naked and sail away with him. That's what he wants. Pfft, old fart."

"I think he's sweet. Fact, I'm gonna go see what he has for sale today." I stood and stretched.

"If he's got any mussels, would you mind grabbing me a bag? I'll pay you back." Jeanine got up and turned for the house.

"It's my treat, really. You guys have had me over several times and now you gave me a lesson on being woo woo."

"We prefer the term witchy." Heloise blew out a last puff of smoke and winked. "I'm excited about Tuesday. We haven't had anyone join us for a moon party in a *looong* time."

"Thanks for the pep talk. I'll get to work on that list ASAP."

I hugged Heloise and headed off, feeling a thousand times better. Already, Emily's call and Weasel's weaselly ways felt like a passing storm in my rearview mirror. It was just a house, and this summer was just a transition. And soon, I wouldn't have to worry about any of it anymore.

10

"Ahoy, there!" I ran onto the beach, waving my arms.

Salty Sid's whistly tune became shouts of today's catch. "Jumbo shrimp, dolphin, lobster…" He approached my stretch of beach and stopped ringing his bell when he spotted me. "Miss Lily of the Lilliputians!" he called in the voice of a royal statesman.

First a Pulitzer, now a Lilliputian. I wondered how many other new identities I'd pick up while in Skeleton Key.

"How are ya, Sid?"

His blue eyes twinkled. "Still six feet above the surf, kiddo. What can I get ya today?"

"Got any mussels?"

Salty Sid propped one foot up on the edge of his dinghy, rolled up his T-shirt sleeve, exposing—no joke—an anchor tattoo like Popeye. He flexed his bicep. "How 'bout them mussels? Eh?" He flashed a row of crooked teeth.

"Quite impressive, but I'm looking for the bearded kind that taste delicious with wine sauce."

Salty Sid's shoulder deflated in mock rejection. "I taste terrible with wine sauce. But let's see what I got in my magic cooler today." With dramatic flair, he propped it open and produced a pound-bag of mussels. "For Jeanine. Am I right?"

"Yes, thank you, and I'll take one lobster, a bag of jumbo shrimp, and a buzzsaw."

"What's the saw for?" He gave me a sidelong glance.

"To buzz off my head, Sid. I've had a shitty day."

"Let me guess. The weasel again."

"Good guess."

The foot propped up again, and now a pointed finger entered the stance. "Listen. You tell that no-good son of a bitch to leave you alone. You tell him that *I* said that he can go dunk his head in a piranha cesspool if he doesn't, and if he still gives you crap, you give him my email."

"Whoa."

"SaltySid@eatmyfist.com," he said, flexing his anchor tattoo again.

"I'll be sure to tell him." I giggled. If only Salty Sid knew that Weasel was 6'3", in perfect shape, and could take him with one hand behind his back.

"He may be tall and in perfect shape, but I'll take him, that's for flippin' sure."

"Wait...how did you do that?"

"Do what?"

"Never mind." I swore the residents and I were on the same bandwidth sometimes. "Venmo again?" I pulled out my phone to fire off a payment, but Sid was still on his soapbox.

"I'm tired of losers giving women shit. They should try walking in you girls's shoes sometimes. Am I right? Let them try having babies, or taking care of a house all alone with small children, or having their monthly periods..."

"Okay...okay..." I held up a hand. He didn't have to go all old-school cavalier on me.

"Or dealing with catcalls, or unwanted sexual advances, harassment in the workplace, harassment *out* of the workplace, 'you should smile more,' and other stupid things we tell women."

I glanced up from my phone at him.

"Lower salaries, the tampon tax, pink razors that cost more...why are we punishing women for being women?"

"I...I mean, I agree."

He ticked off on his fingers. "Uneven access to education, lack of political representation, gender inequalities. The list goes on and on, Lily."

"Exactly," I whispered. "It does."

"And that's without racism, ageism, or discrimination toward marginalized women added to the mix. When does it end?"

My jaw dropped. Not an ounce of insincerity leaked from his pores. Salty Sid's face had turned beet red. The dude was earnest in his convictions. I could only stare at him and blink.

Suddenly, as if snapping from a trance, he waved a hand. "Listen to me, blathering on. Yellowtail?" He held up a fish.

"Uh...no, thanks. Still have some frozen from last time, but thanks for lending an ear, Sid. You're quite literally the best. Don't know if anyone's ever told you that."

"Anytime, doll. Anytime." He motored off on his dinghy again, ringing his bell, whistling his sailor tune, waving at the empty beach as he left. Look at him with his life together with so little. *Be more like Sid,* I thought.

I trudged up the sand, stopping to kick aside more of it off the wooden bike path. I couldn't tell where the border was, but the boardwalk was pretty wide. I wondered, if Atlantis Cruise Line ended up buying the island, if they would uncover the whole thing, tear it up, or refurbish it. The idea of them razing what currently existed here did make me sad.

I dropped the seafood off at my fridge, the mussels at Jeanine's, then came home to a nice tall glass of holy shit. What a day. First things first. After kayaking under the sun and with the memory of Weasel's text war fresh on my mind, I absolutely had to shower.

As steaming water pelted my body, I remembered Heloise's advice to let the negative of the past "wash away." I tried to imagine Weasel and all his antagonistic antics vacating my brain, swirling down the drain with the rest of the salt, sweat, and stress. I had to let go.

Afterwards, I threw on a T-shirt with no bra, a pair of sleep shorts, and twisted my hair into a messy top bun, then proceeded to my happy place. In the kitchen, Bowie, knowing the drill, jumped onto the counter to watch. "Hey, bud. Wanna help me prep a big, ol' lobster?"

Bowie said yes. I gave him a good ol' scritch.

Turning on a playlist of chill music, I poured a glass of red wine and got to work making creamy risotto with lemon parmesan sauce. Needing some rosemary from my beautiful new herb patch, I flicked on the light and ducked out the side door. Jumpin' jellybeans, something had changed.

Over the last two days, seemed the garden had fluffed out. Plants stood with more confidence, if that even made any sense, and the hibiscus bushes were smiling. I know that sounds insane, they were just plants, but where a bramble of nearly dead foliage sat imprisoned, awaiting death before, now new life emerged.

WITCH OF KEY LIME LANE

"Hello, beautiful." I took a quick walk through the side yard, running my hands through all the vegetation, giving all the plants a high five. At the herb garden, I smiled, twisted a sprig of rosemary off its stalk, and noticed the top quarter of the mermaid fountain smiling back at me with that guarded Mona Lisa smile.

"Hey, you. I'm going to paint you soon. And you, thank you for the rosemary," I said to the plant, then went back inside.

There was a knock. And me, braless and dressed in rags. Whatever, not like it mattered. When I opened the door, two, old light fixtures jutted into my face, electrical wires dangling like entrails from the hands of a highly (and inconveniently) statuesque boat captain.

"I snagged these at a garage sale. Want 'em?"

"But don't you? I assume that's why you bought them." I was grateful to the lanterns for having something to look at besides the captain. Although…I supposed stealing a look or two wouldn't hurt. He had to know he was a Renaissance statue.

"I can take one, you can take one. Which one you want?" He modeled them like Vanna White.

"Both are pretty." One was antique polished brass, the other white metallic with a crackled finish. "I think I like the antique brass one better."

"Dang it, that one was mine," Jax chided.

"Then you take it!"

"I'm kidding." A wide smile split his sunny cheeks into a perfectly symmetrical face. "I knew you'd pick that one. It'll look nice out front. Want me to install it?"

"If you want to, but don't feel like you have to help me."

"I want to do it."

"Well, okay then."

He peeked his head in. "Dude, something smells amazing. Of course, something smells amazing. It's Lily Blanchett cooking. What is my life?"

I definitely felt a flush of heat rising into my cheeks, and I was strongly aware of how little I was wearing, how haphazard my hair probably looked. At least I didn't smell like seaweed.

"Have you eaten?" I gestured toward the food. "There's plenty for one more."

"I wouldn't want to impose," he said, setting the front door light on the patio floor. If he was trying to look dejectedly bashful but hungry at the same time, he was doing an excellent job.

"Come in. Not imposing at all. We can't let Sid's seafood go to waste, and it's only me." I felt bad for the way that came out. It wasn't like I was inviting him in only so food wouldn't go to waste. "What I mean is, I'd be happy to feed you. I mean, I'd be happy to share."

My neck felt hot. Now would not be a good time for a hot flash. Good lord, why couldn't I have a normal conversation with a good-looking man and not wear my pheromones on my sleeve like a horny cougar?

Because you're a normal, experienced woman with needs. Nothing wrong with that.

It could've been my own voice, or someone else's. I didn't care anymore. I'd already gotten used to the idea of someone watching over me.

Without a hat, Jax ran a hand through his thick, shiny hair. "Have you invited anyone else for dinner yet? Wait. Scratch that. Not what I meant." Pretending to slap his own face, he tried again with a less nosy-sounding question.

"What I mean is, have you invited Heloise or Jeanine to one of your coveted, five-star Michelin meals, or am I the first?" He winced at his own words.

Guess I wasn't the only one mortified by my rusty flirting skills. "Not yet, no." I laughed.

"Yes." He pulled in a victorious fist. "Suckers!"

The water had begun to boil, and the sauce was ready to simmer. I let the lobster slide into the pot and pulled out a few jumbo shrimp to add, now that I had a guest. Bowie slinked out of hiding to sniff Jax's feet then quickly leaned into his fingers.

"Oh, hey, cutie. You're a lucky one."

Bowie, without shame whatsoever, rolled onto his back and purred loudly.

"Yeah, I hear you," Jax said. "You get to live here with this talented cottage witch, cooking up all sorts of amazing smells and tastes. No wonder you're a fat kitty. That's right, belly, belly, belly."

His rubbing of Bowie's tummy made me smile.

But uh… "Cottage witch? What is that?" It wasn't that I objected to being called a cottage witch, it's that I had no clue what that even was.

"Oh, you've never heard of that term?"

"You have?" Although, with a boat named *Sea Witch*, maybe he knew more about witches than I did. "I thought witches were green, warty, and put spells on people."

Jax side-eyed me. "Come on, you know that's not true." He reconsidered. "Don't you?"

I got the sense there was something I was supposed to know but hadn't been let in on a secret. All I could do was stir the sauce, questioning all I ever thought I knew about life.

"Your aunt was a cottage witch," he said, breaking the silence. "You know, a woman into her home, cooking, decorating, making hearth magic. Men loved her—ovens feared her."

"I've never even heard of that."

"So, I just shoved my foot in my mouth?"

"Seems that way."

"I only said it because that's what Sylvie used to call herself all the time. She'd say, 'Now don't you go irking this ol' cottage witch, Jax,' whenever I'd leave her gate open by accident. Maybe it was metaphorical?"

I thought of the items I'd found in the house so far—crystals, candles, journals… It was entirely possible that I never knew my Aunt Sylvie that well. If she had considered herself a cottage witch, I had to know more before I lost her.

Did Jeanine and Heloise know? Did Sid?

"Fat boy. Fatty fat fat. Belly, belly…" Jax continued to play with Bowie. I got the sense he wanted me to drop the subject.

"He's Rubenesque, not fat. Remember that."

"I bet he gets all the ladies with those eyes. What are those, aquamarines and emeralds installed in his head? Jeez."

"Aren't they beautiful? Heterochromia," I said, but I couldn't stop thinking about Sylvie being a cottage witch.

"Hence his name—David Bowie."

"I'm impressed. Hey, I'm throwing in extra shrimp for you just for knowing that."

"Seems like my luck is on a roll," he said, leaning against the counter and crossing his arms.

For a minute, he watched me cook. I could feel his eyes following every move I made. I wasn't used to this, and to be honest, I felt more than a little off my game. I hadn't made any effort to look nice for company, and with this gorgeous man staring at me, it only made me self-conscious about the cellulite on the back of my thighs, how un-perky my boobs must've looked under this shirt, and the twenty pounds I still needed to lose.

Stop it.

You look lovely.

Before I knew it, I started thumbing through my phone between sauce stirs to keep my eyes off him, when I really wanted to meet his gaze head on. Nothing wrong with getting back in the game.

I cleared my throat. "The garden looks great today. A thousand times better than before. Thank you, for all that trimming you did. It must've spurred new growth."

"Oh?" He slid closer to watch the lobster and shrimp finish boiling. I could smell his sunbaked skin. Mixed with the wine and fragrant scent of rosemary—intoxicating. "It was long-neglected."

I couldn't look up from the screen. I knew if I did, he'd be looking at me with those moss-green eyes, and I'd be forced with the decision on how I wanted this conversation to go. Did I really want to flirt with a man who was giving me attraction vibes? My divorce wasn't final yet, and something about that nagged at me.

Why wasn't it final? And what would I have to do to make it *be* final? Not fighting the house, for one. Giving up, letting Derek win. Clearly, I wasn't ready to move on. I couldn't even talk to Jax without thinking of my divorce.

"Jax…"

"I didn't mean it that way." He shook his head. "I know how that must've sounded. I was, in all honesty, talking about the garden. It's been sitting there for years. It needed attention. I felt bad because I could've trimmed it years ago."

"It's okay. I appreciate it."

"It's just, and I know how this will sound, but you give off Sylvie energy. I know you're not her, but you remind everyone of her with your cooking, gardening, and all. From the moment you got here, you've been bringing this house back to life."

"I…"

Screw it, just do it—look at him. I put the phone down and looked up. How unfair was it that some men's lashes were longer and thicker than our own?

"I feel guilty," I blurted. "There, I said it. You should know that I didn't know my aunt very well. I only visited her every blue moon since she moved to the ALF, and now the more I get to know about her through you, Heloise, Sid, Jeanine…the more I regret it."

"I'm sorry. I didn't mean to dredge up bad feelings."

"You haven't. It's the opposite. Now, I feel like there's this whole side of my family I didn't know about. It makes me wonder what else could be buried inside of me, you know? For the last two years, I've been feeling like there's something just under the surface. Like I haven't quite reached my full potential."

"Which is pretty amazing, considering all you've accomplished so far."

"Exactly. It's an odd feeling, knowing a well of latent possibilities lives inside of you, but never accessing it, and that's where I am now, Jax."

"I think that's freaking amazing."

"But you coming here sets my thoughts off in a hundred different directions, and this might sound presumptuous, and I apologize in advance for that if it does…"

"No need to apologize, Lily. Or to preface anything you say. Or to say anything at all. I came here unannounced. I make you uncomfortable. I can go. I say that in the most guilt-free way. Okay?" He backed up for the door.

"No, please. I'm not telling you to leave."

He paused.

"Just to listen. I need to say something." Looking at the ceiling a moment to gather my courage, I dove in. "I'm not looking for a relationship right now. That sounds even crazier out loud, but I just needed to put that out there. You're super nice, you've helped me so much since I've gotten here, and please don't get me wrong, I don't want you to stop doing those things either. It's nice. Really nice."

"But it's too much. I get it. I'll back off."

"That's just it. It's actually just the right amount, and to be honest, I love hanging out with you. But…" Wow, where was all of this coming from? "It's just a confusing time for me. I feel like I have to finish one thing before I start another. Discover myself first. Does that make sense?"

Aren't things already finished?

"I get it, Lil. The last thing I want to do is to confuse you. I only want to be friends. It's not easy being the only person my age on this block, so when you arrived, I thought, 'Finally, someone to talk to.' I'll be honest, too, you're more gorgeous in person, and I can't stop staring at you, but it's not why I'm here."

The thought lingered between us. The words wouldn't form on my lips. He tapped my arm. "I interrupted what you were saying. Sorry about that."

Words I'd never heard Weasel use before. Apologizing for interrupting? "It's okay."

"What were you saying?"

"What you just said. Let's be friends. Please?"

That would take the pressure off our obvious physical attraction long enough to think about what I needed. I could hear legions of women my age booing me, telling me to go for it. The guy was obviously into me.

But I needed time.

"Of course. That sounds perfect. Thanks for saying so, Lil." He clapped once and looked through the cabinets, getting to work, grabbing plates and utensils, even napkins. "I'll set the table?"

"Thanks." I let out a huge sigh. I was pretty proud of myself for how I handled that. A load lifted off my shoulders. Now we could hang without complicated emotions in the way. He was still hot, and I was still conflicted, but at least I had a smile on my face, a vast improvement from earlier today.

11

At three in the morning, I still couldn't sleep. Snippets from the evening kept replaying in my mind on a cycle loop. Like Sylvie being a cottage witch, or Jax's idea that I reminded him of her. How I needed to go visit her before things got worse. The guilt that weighed on me because I hadn't done that.

Echoes of things I didn't know nagged at me.

My eyes felt like they were opening after a long sleep.

New stuff I'd learned about Jax stuck with me, too, like his job as a charter boat captain being a dream, his mother was a Cuban exile, which meant she'd fled Cuba as a child during the revolution of the 60s. His father had been a "Conch," what they called local residents of the Keys.

Each time Jax had cast his eyes upward to think of something, my eyes had caught the reddish-brown stubble of his five o'clock shadow. The more wine I drank, the more I observed him, like the way his eyes rolled into the back of his head after the first bite of food I'd made, or the way his rather large hand wrapped about the ice-cold bottle of beer.

Not to dwell on the obvious, but Jax was beautiful to look at, though I kept hoping he wasn't checking me out the same way, or he'd surely notice the wrinkles around my eyes or the stubble on my legs. As the night went on, however, I stopped caring, and we had a good time. He talked to me with respect, so polar opposite from Weasel. Jax was a whole new vibe.

I'd be lying if I said I wasn't tipsy by the end of the night and considered kissing him at the door as he was leaving, despite everything I told him. The two halves of my brain were at war with each other. One half said, "Not yet," and the other screamed, "Go on, girl! You traveled down to have fun and relax, didn't you?"

Yes, but I wasn't Weasel. *I* waited until a relationship was officially over before moving on. At this point, I wasn't even sure I'd like another romantic relationship ever again. Done. Been there, bought the too-expensive photo package.

It was getting late. I really had to sleep. Deep breaths and soft music were in order. I kicked off the old comforter, which folded over a snoring cat, who didn't even flinch. I played binaural beats on my phone, readjusted myself, and tried to purge my thoughts.

I am tired…

I am sleepy…

Poor Jax's son hadn't come to visit him in two months. I felt bad that his business wasn't booming the way he'd hoped either. Before he'd left, I'd spent an hour showing him websites that made web design super easy. Also, how Instagram worked and a few influencers he should follow.

"I don't want to spend all my time on the computer," he'd said. "I just want customers to find me when they're passing through."

"It doesn't work that way anymore," I'd said, feeling a bit frustrated that he wouldn't take my suggestions to heart.

As a businesswoman, it was maddening to see a smart guy like him unable to wrap his head around a few simple steps to improve his business' performance. But it wasn't my problem, I reminded myself.

"Ugh, go to sleep!" I called out in the stillness, plucking my shirt to get some air circulating. How did Aunt Sylvie manage with such a crappy air conditioner?

Finally, I peeled off my shirt and let the ceiling fan cool me down.

I am tired…

I am sleepy…

I am having hot flashes…

Hello, perimenopause. Boo to you, too. Restless leg syndrome didn't help either. I kept kicking and kicking my legs. I had just managed to stop fidgeting a minute when the window in the bedroom popped up an inch.

I gasped and sat up. "Who's there?"

I knew it got breezy on the beach at night, but exactly how does a window move up by itself? With it cracked open, I heard the whooshing of the ocean, the wind cooing through the gap, chimes tinkling somewhere. Off in the distance, the slow rumble of thunder warned of rain and the notes of 1940s music filtered through the house as if coming from another space and time.

"Okayyy."

I stared at the ceiling fan. I should have felt scared, but a) it was probably the wind which had caught the window from underneath, b) music drifted on the wind from other people's houses, and c) I wasn't afraid of ghosts. There was no negative energy in this house. Whoever made things move around was benevolent. The atmosphere felt peaceful, not to mention a *lot* cooler than it had a moment ago.

Whoever was here understood hot flashes.

"Thank you," I said aloud.

Still, I was wide awake, and the sounds of Glenn Miller's *In the Mood* from someone's house or boat called to me. It wasn't every day I had a backyard beach all to myself. Back home, I never would've gone outside at three in the morning to take in the sweet smell of storms in the distance, but I wasn't home. And I wasn't the old me anymore.

I liked who I was becoming.

My feet hit the floor. I navigated through the dark house, holding onto walls and stair rails, feeling in some ways, like I was sleepwalking. The kitchen and living room were dark and smelled of fresh paint. My peripheral vision caught movement, but it was just the white curtain blowing over another open window. Same one that'd been open when I first arrived.

Someone liked their windows open, and it wasn't me.

The song ended, and the music stopped altogether.

Through the side door, out the gate, I stepped onto the sand, still warm from the sun's heat. I walked all the way to the water's edge and sat in the sand, letting the waves pool around me. Yes, I was topless, but no one was around on the lonely stretch of beach, and it occurred to me right then how I hadn't swum in the ocean yet. In the ten days I'd been here, I hadn't bathed on the beach.

What kind of vacationer was I?

The workaholic kind.

My voice or not, it was true.

In just my underwear, I waded in. It was warmer than I expected, like a calming bath for my weary body. In the distance, red pinpoints of light marked the horizon, but other than that, the only lights were the millions of stars in the dark sky. Along the beach, palms trees swayed and rustled. To the north, the glow of Miami reminded me that civilizations still existed, but everywhere else—darkness.

The universe was smiling down.

The enormity of it, the awe that I might even have a place in it, felt like a miracle. From the sky, I looked like nothing. A speck of dirt swimming in the ocean. Weasel was nobody. Our celebrity friends were nobodies. That we had busy lives and argued about stuff felt like a fluke. How silly that we spent so much time thinking about ourselves, about furthering our lives, reaching for dreams, when we were star flakes at best.

Why were we here?

To experience moments like this. To find the gemstones in time and let go of the rest. Let go—that had been my homework, assigned by my two witchy neighbors. To make a list and put down everything on it I wished to say goodbye to, remove everything that didn't serve me anymore. Get rid of anything that didn't lift my vibration, and all that woo-woo stuff.

Except it didn't feel like woo-woo right now. I understood it. What would I put on my Letting Go List?

Weasel, for one. Stop caring what he was doing, what he was telling our shared friends, my in-laws, who hadn't reached out once, by the way. I could hear it now: *Lily didn't know how to have fun. Lily was a workaholic. Lily didn't have time for me. It was all Lily's fault. If I hadn't been so unhappy with Lily, I wouldn't have sought out an extramarital relationship.*

Bullshit. I had to stop caring what others thought about me. I had to accept that our marriage hadn't ended in a way I would have liked. Things ended embarrassingly. That was out of my control.

Next, I had to let go of *Chelsea Garden Grill*.

Yes, I created it. Yes, it grew into TV fame because of all the hard work I put in. Yes, the cheerful energy of the eatery owed itself to me, because I'd put my customers first. I'd helped design it, furnish it, given it that trendy-but-casual NYC vibe. It was what it was because of me. Even Weasel had admitted that a thousand times in interviews before we split. Suddenly, he'd stopped giving me credit.

I was losing *Chelsea Garden Grill*, like it or not, and this, I realized, made me sadder than losing Derek. However, I'd done it once before, I could do it again with a new restaurant. A new place would be even better, encompass a new style, new menu, new aesthetic. Maybe I'd finally open one of those trendy Halloween restaurants where cauldrons bubbled with the Soup of the Day. I'd get to make design choices I hadn't been able to before without Derek there to nix them. I could open anywhere, not just the City. The suburbs would be great. Wouldn't that be nice? To stumble out of bed and roll down the street to my new kitchen space?

Next—the house.

Heloise and Jeanine were totally right on this. Even if Derek conceded and let me keep the house, why would I want to stay there? To be tortured by memories? Christmases, Halloweens, family BBQs, our wine cellar, the weekend we built the fireplace, the sunken living room, the kitchen, and so on.

Long ago, my mother had a Billy Joel album that she loved listening to, and this one lyric always stuck with me.

Life is a series of hellos and goodbyes. I'm afraid it's time for goodbye again... As a child, I remembered wondering if that was true, if saying goodbye was a big part of life. It didn't seem possible then. Life was shiny and new, the whole world ahead of me. Until Gary left us, I hadn't been faced with too many partings. But now that I was older, I understood the deeper meaning of that lyric.

Celebrities I'd adored as a teen were dying. My parents' friends were getting old or sick and passing. Common friends had split up, and I had to choose which side to stay in touch with. Aunt Sylvie sat in an ALF, waiting for her time. Billy Joel was right.

There was, of course, a lot more to add to the list, like letting go of the fact that I'd never look twenty again, that wrinkles were a thing now, that crow's feet around my eyes were here to stay, that the extra twenty-five pounds I'd picked up over the last ten years weren't going anywhere without starving myself.

But in its place were wisdom, a new attitude, not giving a shit. Doing things my way. Look at me, wading in Mother Ocean's embrace at four in the morning practically nude. There was beauty in that, too, and I planned on exploring this side of me more from now on.

After a while, I reached for the sky and hugged it. "Thanks for the chat," I told the universe. With a smile, I waded out of the water and headed back inside.

12

New Moon Day.

Out front, Captain Jax installed the lantern. I let him. Nothing wrong with having a man around, especially when that man knew when to stay out of the way or wanted to make things better.

I'd gone and bought another gallon of light gray paint for the kitchen and gotten to work on whitewashing the old wood cabinets. It might've been too much gray, too neutral a color, but it eased my anxieties, so I liked it. During a break, I sat outside in the garden with a glass of lemonade, wide-brimmed hat on my head, while Bowie cleaned his tail.

I worked on my Letting Go List, adding more stuff I'd thought of in the morning, stuff like, *Accept that Carmen will stay to work with Weasel, Let go of outcomes,* and *Stop being defensive.*

Because Weasel was always taking, I'd found myself over the last year clinging to things I never cared about that much before, for the simple fact that he was taking it. I didn't like who I'd become. Yes, it was important to stand up for myself, but to what end? The only way I would ever truly heal was to let go of outcomes. Whatever happened happened.

A face peered over the fence. "Done. Wanna see?" Captain Jax's eyebrows wiggled.

"Be right there." As I headed in, I whistled at Bowie. "Come on, bud."

Bowie had stopped cleaning to stare out into the garden, flare his nostrils, and give a mini-hiss. I followed his gaze to the mermaid, no longer covered by bushes. Now she was free to watch us intently, and that made both me and Bowie feel unnerved at times. But it wasn't the mermaid Bowie was looking at. It was Luna, big golden eyes watching us from the key lime trees.

"We see you over there," I said. "You might think you're all stealth, but you're not."

Bowie refused to come in, so I left him in the garden while I went to check out Jax's work. He switched places with me at the door, where he could flip the light switch on and off.

"Oh, wow! That looks fantastic!" It really did. Jax had done a great job of polishing the antique brass and making it look like new.

"Notice the highlights? I hand-painted those." He beamed with pride.

The lantern sparkled with a shiny copper along the ridges. They didn't even look like they'd been painted by hand. "I love the bulb you put in."

"Gives it a witchy flicker, doesn't it?" He looked up at his work. "Like a gas one my mother used to have."

"Yes, kind of pirate-y. I like it."

"Pirate-y. Perfect word," he agreed. "I'm going to pull out a few old nails and replace that rotten section at the end over there, if you want."

"I owe you tremendously. Just tell me how much, and I'll happily send you a payment, Jax." It occurred to me then that he might be putting in all this hard work for money, but I didn't want to offend him in case he wasn't.

"Nothing. Really, it's no big deal. It keeps me busy, and I have all the materials. Seriously. You're helping me enough with all the marketing advice."

"That you're not taking." I laughed.

"Bah. I'll give them a shot."

"Hey, that's better than what you said last night. What was it again? 'I suck at business?'"

Fear of failure perplexed me. I never understood people who didn't take risks to make the only life they had a better one, and last night, Jax had bordered on apathy, but I also knew people got stuck in their ways, including me.

He shrugged. "Nah, that wasn't me. I don't say embarrassingly wimpy things in front of successful women who also happen to be kind and gorgeous. Anyway, onto those nails."

"Hey, Jax?"

"Yep."

"Were you playing music last night? Like old-timey music?"

"I was watching *Captain America* on mute. Why?"

"Never mind." It had to have come from another house.

I watched him work for a short while, went back to finishing the kitchen, which looked like a completely new space, and removed the old country curtains hanging in the window. Immediately, the house had a more modern feel to it, and I felt my nerves melting away.

In the evening, I took my list, a white candle I'd found in a box upstairs, plus a lighter, and headed out. The sun was descending, boats were gathered in the bay, and performers belting out Jimmy Buffett songs could be heard across the sundown bars for miles.

I chose a small fishing bridge off the neighboring island of Tavernier, walking out to the middle, facing the sunset. First, I lit the candle, melted the end, and got it to stick to the wooden railing. The breeze was a little shifty, so I curled my hand around the flame to protect it from blowing out.

Then I let out a huge breath.

"Universe, if you're listening, here are some things I need help letting go. Firstly, Derek Blanchett," I said his name aloud. Not sure if the universe knew who "Weasel" was, and I wanted to make sure it found the right person.

His name brought me pain. Unexpectedly, the tears came. I thought I'd cried all there were to cry, but apparently, I had a whole reservoir.

"This wasn't what I signed up for, but I know that bad stuff happens to good people all the time, and I can cry about it, or I can pick up and move on. I understand things will never be the same again. It's probably better this way. The old will clear a path for the new."

What would be "the new?" At times, I wish I had a crystal ball so I could find out.

"Anyway, he's not my problem anymore." With that, I stuck the corner of the paper into the flame and waited as it curled and blackened between my fingertips. "Goodbye, Derek." I threw the bits of paper into the gulf. I did the same with all the other strips of paper I'd brought along, saying goodbye to the things holding me back, tossing them off the bridge. They twirled away, carried off by the current.

When I was done, I let out another deep breath and watched the sun set below the horizon, imagining that it was taking my strips of paper and pain and frustration with it, never to be seen again. Cheers erupted from the boats. I imagined them just for me.

I definitely felt lighter. If only I could carry this feeling every day at every moment, whenever I needed it most. Plucking the candle off the railing, I noticed many more splotches of wax along the wood. Seemed I wasn't alone and would never be.

Like the kayak ride, I got more comfortable with the idea of doing things alone, so I stopped at a tiki bar on the way back. Why not?

Ordering a rumrunner, I watched a group of women my age on the dock, celebrating with a round of drinks. One of them wore a silky caftan like Mrs. Roper from *Three's Company*, except her hair was long and blond, her vibe was joyous, filled with I Don't Give a F*ck energy, as she danced barefoot while her friends cheered her on.

I envied Caftan Lady. I envied her so much, I pulled out my phone, selected a yellow caftan from Amazon right there, and paused when I arrived at the shipping page. The preset had my Long Island address, of course, which didn't look right and never would again, but the item would take 7-8 days to arrive, and I wasn't sure I'd be in Skeleton Key that long.

Do it. You have nothing to lose, Lily.

I made a decision. I would have the clothing sent to 111 Key Lime Lane anyway. There was no real home to go back to, and I could use another week or two in the Keys. *Thanks, Caftan Lady.* I watched her toast her friends with her margarita high in the air, and for a moment, I thought she saw me watching and winked.

Back at the house, I smiled when I saw the new porch light welcoming me back. Jax was long gone, his boat missing from the canal, but sitting on the porch, waiting for me was Luna. With the house reflecting the light of a gorgeous sunset, a golden-eyed cat sitting on the front steps, and a new light fixture, I pulled out my camera phone and framed the shot. Ghost cat or not, she came with the house, and I'd grown to love her.

The photo came out blurry. I deleted it and tried again. Blurry again. I chalked it up to low light and the effects of my rumrunner wearing off. Then I noticed the sign. Wooden, white, with a pretty hand-painted symbol of moon phases on it, it read: *Moon Party, THIS WAY* → The arrow pointed around the side of my house to a craggy path in the beach grass. I followed it toward the hippie sounds of Fleetwood Mac playing off a phone and ladies laughing on the beach.

"There she is!" Heloise widened her arms, extending her gypsy shawl wings. I did a little dance with her.

"Hey, Pulitzer." Jeanine was behind her, looking lovely with her hair in a loose bun, effortless wisps flying away from her face.

Both ladies had a glass of wine in their hands. They'd set up a tent, the kind you find at farmer's markets. "What do you think?" Heloise asked.

Underneath was a six-foot party table decked out with blue and green tablecloths with shiny gold threads, three gold chargers, three ceramic plates with a fishy pattern, battery-powered twinkling lights, a picnic basket, grapes, cheese, a plate of shrimp, wine bottles, a deck of Tarot cards, crystals, and lots and lots of other magical ornaments hanging everywhere. Further out in the sand was a firepit, crackling with steady flames.

"This is so beautiful!" I pressed my hands together.

"We don't usually get this fancy," Jeanine said.

"Oh, she lies like a viper. We always get this fancy!" Heloise laughed. "We just got a little extra fancy for you."

"Aww, thanks, guys. This means the world to me!" I hugged them both. "I burned my Letting Go List, like you told me. Sorry I'm not naked."

Jeanine guffawed. "There's time yet. Come here, girl, let's get this party started."

I may have run a 5-star restaurant back home, but these women took the award for best homemade meals. Shrimp scampi, lobster bisque, conch fritters, and yep, no party in Skeleton Key would be complete without a key lime pie.

"You take such good care of others," Heloise said, clinking her glass to mine. "It's time someone took care of you!"

Her words unleashed something inside of me, and a waterfall of tears spilled forth. For a long time, Heloise and Jeanine sat on either side of me, consoling me. Rarely did anyone ever acknowledge how hard I worked or tried. Amazing how just hearing those simple words could make me feel better.

Over the next two hours, we ate, drank, and laughed our asses off. The fairy lights twirled in my vision, the firepit flames crackled as they spit into the air, and on more than one occasion, Heloise and Jeanine cackled like real witches. We never got naked in the physical sense, but it seemed like we bared everything.

"And now…" Heloise declared, tripping over her own feet, then laughing as she recovered. "We initiate Ms. Lily Blanchett into our moon party shenanigans!" She raised her glass toward the moonless night.

"Into our coven," Jeanine mock-whispered, hooted, then polished off her wine.

I raised my glass in camaraderie. I always thought of witches as women who hexed others, but Heloise and Jeanine were teaching me new things every day. Apparently, you could form friendships with other women to celebrate aging, commiserate, commune with nature, and force change through ritual and everyday practice, and also be considered a witch.

If that was being a witch, I was all for it.

"Look at me, Aunt Sylvie!" I twirled in the sand. "I'm a cottage witch!" I twirled so hard, I fell on my ass.

I had no clue what made me say that but hearing Heloise and Jeanine cheer in jubilation and echo my words, "a cottage witch!" made my wounded heart feel a thousand times better. Plus, for just a moment, I felt connected to Aunt Sylvie, like I actually knew her for once.

Around the firepit, Heloise and Jeanine danced, did something called "calling the quarters," where they spoke aloud to the east, south, west, and north, thanking them for direction, and raised their arms to the moonless, starry sky. Waves tickled my feet, then retreated like laughing children, as I watched these amazing women harness spirits of the earth.

Once upon a time, I would've found the whole thing too weird. Why were we thanking winds of the east? What did "as above, so below" even mean? Heloise said we were raising energy, but I didn't see any change. I felt them, though—

GABRIELLE KEYES

big changes on the precipice, like tonight was like another time and place. Like I was a different Lily, living a parallel life. It made me want to rip off my old exterior and throw on a new one. Maybe that's what Jeanine meant by getting naked.

Either way, it solidified my decision to stay at Aunt Sylvie's a while longer. Another week or two, but then I really did have to start a planning a fresh start. In my fevered state, I may or may not have announced my intention to stay aloud, and the ladies may or may not have whooped, hollered, and pulled me into their dance circle, telling me it was the best news they'd heard all day. And for just a few hours, I forgot about the misery that had led me to this magical island and instead, basked in the joy that it had.

13

A fat cat purred warm kitty breath into my ear. I rubbed my eyes. The angle of the sun felt wrong. I grabbed my phone. 1:06 PM. "What the?" I shot up in bed, dumping Bowie into the space between the headboard and mattress.

Indignantly, he crawled out and shot straight from the room. A moment later, he was meowing downstairs. I rubbed my temples and dragged myself to the bathroom.

What had I done last night?

Ah, yes. The moon party with Jeanine and Heloise. Now, that had been eye-opening. And the work they'd put into the menu and decorations were, as usual, chef's kiss. Those two were the epitome of professional-quality outdoor dining. Why Jeanine and Heloise weren't running a catering company, hosting a hundred beach weddings a year, was beyond me.

After getting ready for the day, my phone rang, displaying a name I hadn't seen in a while—Chase. "Well, hello, offspring!"

"Hey, Mom. What's up?" His voice was flat.

"What's up with you?"

"Nothing, Dean went to his girlfriend's house, so I'm just here, chillin'."

"Chillin' like a villain?" I snorted. What good was it being a mother if I couldn't embarrass my kids?

"Something like that. Where are you, Mom?"

"In the Keys. I told you. I've sent you like twenty photos since I've been here. Do you not check your texts?"

"I do. What I mean is, why are you still there? I thought you were only going for a week. It's been, like, all of June."

"Chase, it's been two weeks. It just feels like all of June, because your term ended, and now you've got nothing to distract you. Do you want to come down and stay with me for a while?"

"What? No." He sounded put off. I could almost hear him reply, *I want you here, where I can count on you.* "I thought you'd be back by now. When are you coming home?"

Home. What an interesting word.

"Actually, babe, I'm probably going to stay another week or so. I've been fixing up Aunt Sylvie's house to possibly rent or sell it, and it's taking a little longer than I thought."

"What about the restaurant? What about the house?"

"The house is fine. Bowie's here with me. And your dad's taking care of the grill."

"What do you mean? You don't work there anymore?"

I sighed. "Honey, no. I hate to say it, but I don't. Your father is asking for the restaurant, so I'm kind of in transition right now, figuring out where to go from here."

"But that's where you work. Where you've worked for twenty years. He can't just throw you onto the street. You weren't the one who decided to leave the family and start another one. He should be the one leaving to start his own restaurant, Mom. You have to fight for *Chelsea Grill.*"

"Chase..." I stared out the window. Sparkling aquamarine ocean with a rainstorm on the horizon. "It's not worth fighting over. I can just as easily start a new restaurant."

"What? Do you even hear yourself? That's not the point. Dude, you just said *Chelsea Garden Grill isn't* worth fighting for. I don't understand you, bro."

"Bro," I retorted. "It's not for you to understand. Your father's image is connected to the grill. If he loses the grill, he loses his brand." Even though the show was cancelled because of the restraining order, he still needed something to survive, and the man *did* have small children now.

"Who fucking cares, Mom? What do you care what he loses? You're letting him win. Make him go out and start his own restaurant. He can call it *Traitor's Bar and Grill*, or *Asshole's Tavern*."

I bit back tears. Hearing my son so angry at his father brought all the pain pouring back in again.

"Stand your ground, Mom. You put that restaurant on the map. That place is more yours than it is his, and you know it."

"I know, Chase, but..."

"But what?"

I shook my head. He was right in so many ways. I should be fighting for what was right, what was mine, but good God, I was tired. Of the fighting, the divorce, the stress, and the animosity. I'd just "let go" of it all last night on the bridge under the moonless sky. I just wanted this nightmare to end already. And sure, I supposed I was willing to lose the grill if it meant ending the war.

Call it a sacrifice.

"Chase, I wish it were that easy, but it's more complicated than that. I'm not young, like you. I've been through a lot, I've lived a lot, and now it's time for me to start letting go of things."

"Why are you talking like you're about to die? Dude, your life is just beginning. You should never, ever abandon a battle worth fighting, Mom. Why are you saying this? Who even are you?"

"I…"

I wasn't sure anymore. And there was a lot to unpack here. I knew I wasn't the same person I was a year ago, probably even less that person after living in Skeleton Key for two weeks. Was I becoming soft? It was true that distance had altered how much I thought about my life back in NYC, but had I become one of *those* people? The kind who sailed off on a boat, never to be seen again?

"Chase, I'm happy you called. You're reminding me that I need to resume my responsibilities, and I will. I promise. Your mother has not clocked out forever."

"That part," he said.

"I'm just sorting out a few things out, deciding where I want to go from here. If that means starting a new restaurant just to get rid of the old, or bad, energy, so I can move on…well, I'm willing to do that."

"No, bro, no…"

"It'll be okay, son. Thank you for worrying about me. I really love that part. Like, a lot."

"I just don't like that you're getting shafted."

"I know it's not fair. Thank you. But if you know me at all, you know I won't stay down. I'm hardworking and creative AF, as you kids like to say. And I'm smart. You know that children get their intelligence from their mothers, right?" I smiled through my tears.

I could hear his eyes rolling. "You've said that like ten million times already."

"Good, just didn't want you to forget it. So, starting over with a clean slate may be what I need. Do you have everything you need? Should I transfer money into your account or order you some tacos for tonight?"

"I'll never say no to tacos, but I need my mom is all. I may be old enough to drink, but I still miss you, dude. What the heck. Come home already."

I bit back a sob. I loved my adult-but-still-babies but hated that we were all floating in limbo at the moment. I slapped on my cheery voice. "Thank you, Chase. I love you, too. I'll be back before you know it."

"Give Bowie a belly rub for me," he said.

"I will." I hung up and flopped onto the bed.

Last night, I'd made the choice to release certain things. That hadn't been for show. That had been a solid decision. A commitment to myself. And if I was to feel better and start moving in the right direction for me, I had to stick to it.

After feeding Bowie, I made coffee and grabbed my hat from the hook Jax had installed by the side door and went outside for fresh air. The basil and rosemary had billowed overnight, and the sage and parsley had practically tripled in size. The bougainvillea had changed color with a morning rain, and now, orange and purple blooms dotted the once-abandoned, derelict garden. Even the mermaid seemed to wink at me.

Amazing what love and attention could do.

But I'd made one critical mistake in coming out here. Besides the fact it was a hundred degrees, and I'd brought hot coffee out to drink. I'd brought my phone out as well, and in checking in with the daily news, I went ahead and read a text from Carmen:

I am not a happy camper right now.
I don't know if I should tell you or not.

What is it? What's going on?

Your lovely ex…a.k.a. the Weasel…
hired a new assistant manager
without consulting me. I never
even got to interview the woman
and she already got the job

What?

I nearly chucked my phone across the garden.

Can I call you?

Later. We have a full house.
I'm splitting time between the house
kitchen and the sushi kitchen.

Okay.

My chest heaved like it was going to implode. So much for not letting the Weasel's decisions affect me. Chase was right—he was totally shafting me, shafting everybody, and if I didn't give him a piece of my mind right this second, he would piss all over everything. He already was.

Oh, and the woman he hired?
A friend of Tinder Girl.

                                                    NO.

YES.

"Siri, call Derek."

"Calling…The Weasel."

He answered on the third ring. "Good news travels fast. What are you doing?"

I gritted my teeth.

"What are *you* doing? Since when do you make unilateral decisions regarding the restaurant, Derek?" It was odd—really odd—calling him Derek after years of using "babe" or "love" or "honey."

"Since my business partner shucked her responsibilities and fled to Key Largo."

"It's *shirked*, not shucked, Derek. And you really want to lecture me about responsibilities? Is that where we're going? We're going to talk about people who abandoned their responsibilities in favor of new ones? Are you sure you want to go down that road?" My voice cracked, my heart hurt, and my legs were shaking.

"Lily, I'm not going to rehash this. I doubt you'd want me to think of you as a responsibility, and the kids are in college, for crissake."

"They still need you."

"Apparently, they don't."

"They're angry at you, Derek. Because this is what you do—you go around making decisions for everyone without considering what anyone else feels or wants."

"Lily, you haven't worked at the grill in three weeks."

"Because of *you*, otherwise I'd still be there."

"I didn't ask you to leave."

"Your marital settlement agreement says otherwise."

"Until you sign it, you should be here. And you're not."

"That doesn't give you the right to make decisions for everyone. *You* decided you would keep the restaurant, *you* decided you would keep the house, *you* decided you would break and enter, even though *you* don't live there anymore, and now *you've* unilaterally hired an assistant manager when we always, *always,* make them go through rounds of interviews with all our head chefs and Carmen. When does the reign of terror end?" I screamed.

I had to stop this, or I'd have a heart attack.

"Lily, you and I are the current owners of the restaurant, not Carmen. And if you're not here to make business decisions, as we need a new assistant, as two of our sous-chefs quit last week, well, then I need to make an executive decision."

"I didn't know about the chefs either. Which ones?"

"James and Aldo."

"You could've texted me! Or called me! Just like you did with your girlfriend for several years behind my back. Where there's a will, there's a way, right? How come you were able to talk to her under unfavorable conditions, but then you can't seem to be able to consult me on anything now?"

"That's...really reaching, Lily. I'm busy. I can't do this."

"This is another one of your exploitations of control. Well, you don't get to control me! You don't get to control anyone! You don't get to—"

Suddenly, the phone yanked away from my hand. A tanned finger pressed the red "end" button and my phone went flying over the fence onto the beach. Captain Jax, silent and shirtless, strolled back to the side gate.

"Why did you do that?" I yelled at him. "I've had enough with men thinking they can do whatever they want around me. You don't get to do the same. You hear me?" He kept walking away. "You don't get to do the same!"

"You don't need that stress," Jax called over his shoulder.

I strutted up to him. "Maybe, maybe not. But *I* make the call on when to end a phone call, not you. Not you, got it?" I shoved him with both hands then burst into tears.

Why was I yelling at Captain Jax when he was only trying to do me a favor? Clearly, I needed to disengage from Derek's insanity but was unable to.

Jax held my shoulders then pulled me in for a short hug. "Sorry I threw your phone. But screw that guy. Look what he does to you. I could hear you yelling all the way from my dock." He wiped a tear off my cheek. "You don't need that. You're Lily fucking Blanchett."

Forget that. I was changing my last name the first chance I had.

"What do I need then?" I sobbed, still shaking with anger. "You tell me since you're such an expert."

Mossy green eyes swirled like plankton on calm intracoastal water. For a moment, I thought he was going to bend low and kiss me. At this point, I wouldn't have minded if he bent me over and did more. "Meet me at the boat at 5 AM, and you'll see."

After Jax left, I couldn't quell the rage. I moved from room to room, expending energy, searching and sorting Sylvie's things so I could begin packing them into boxes. According to Mom, Sylvie wouldn't be coming home anytime soon, so I may as well start collecting her things.

In the closet of one of her spare bedrooms, I found a small desk covered in boxes of crap, crap, and more crap. Once I'd removed all the magazines, baskets, and craft materials, I saw it was actually a vanity with a center flap that opened, displaying a mirror.

Inside was a velvety lining filled with pouches, and the drawer underneath it contained all sorts of essential oils, thin candles in every color, wooden matches, tiny glass vials, and coins. Doubloons, like from the pirate days. Several sheets of paper were folded, and inside, in Sylvie's writing, were what seemed to be prayers or petitions for wealth.

For herself, her sister, and especially her niece and nephew, Lily and Gary.

"Oh, Sylvie." I pressed the folded sheets against me and dropped my head. Things hadn't turned out well for Gary, but yes, thank you. For a while there, I did have it all. Starting over was the hardest thing I'd ever had to do. I held the papers close to my chest, imagined Sylvie's prayer coming true again, then put everything back in the drawer.

Picking up one of the pouches, I saw they contained playing cards, except when I pulled them out, they were Tarot cards. Beautiful, gold-foiled cards with dirty, worn edges and elegant, magical images of kings, queens, hierophants, flowers, and animals all flashed up at me. I took the one called Strength with a woman petting a lion and put it in my pocket.

All this time I'd been living in Sylvie's house, and this stuff was sitting here hidden and discarded. In the right drawer were crystals in all different colors, a velvet mat for creating what looked like a grid, a pointy pendulum made of an opaque crystal, and a mini statue of some goddess I couldn't name.

A deep sense of nostalgia for things I didn't understand hit me, and I strongly wished I could learn them. "Tell me all your mysteries, Aunt Sylvie," I whispered.

If you search, you will find, a voice whispered back.

I slammed the drawer and backed away, my heart beating in my chest. Even before I turned, I knew what I would find. Slowly, I twisted around. Luna stood there in Egyptian cat pose.

Bowie had appeared at the door to the room, too, interested to see what she would do next.

I looked at Luna. "Are you…are you talking to me?"

The cat blinked her golden eyes.

"Say something. Just say it, while I'm watching you, so I'll know for sure. I promise I won't freak out."

Luna stood there a whole minute, tentatively watching, but she never spoke. Finally, she stretched, licked her paw, then headed straight for the closet. Shaking, wide awake, completely sober, in awe, I witnessed her duck underneath the vanity and disappear into the ether.

From the doorway, Bowie yawned.

14

Hard to believe a quiet little island could get any quieter, but the stillness at five in the morning was surreal. Without knowing what we were doing today, or where we were going, I packed a small backpack with a few snacks, SPF, my wide-brimmed sun hat, and Sylvie's Tarot deck. The Strength card I'd placed on my nightstand as a reminder.

"See you soon, Bo." I patted the beast's head and slipped out the house. I still couldn't believe what I'd seen yesterday afternoon or the way Bowie simply hadn't cared, like he was used to seeing cats disappear into thin air.

Captain Jax was loading the boat with a medium-sized cooler when I arrived. "Hark! A fair maiden wishes to board the *Sea Witch*. 'Tis bad luck to have a woman on board, I fear."

"Bite me."

"The fair maiden disagrees." He ushered me by the elbow toward the boat's edge. "Just part of my charter boat captain spiel."

"We'll have to work on that then," I said.

"Are you okay?" he asked seriously.

I shrugged. "I don't know. I am, then I'm not. Then I am again."

"Let's get you out on the water," he said. I appreciated his restraint to ask any more questions, because I sure as hell was out of answers.

Captain Jax looked super handsome today. Not that he never did. Clothes-wise, he wore nothing special, but his deep blue T-shirt brought out his eyes, and two-day stubble gave him a rough-hewn look. His nicely formed calves flexed as he stepped on and off the boat, and none of this mattered because we were just friends.

Sigh.

I peered into the canal. "Any manatees today?"

"They come when I wash her down."

"How do they know you're washing her down?"

"They hear the hose water in the canal."

Such incredible, gentle creatures. It broke my heart how so many were killed every year from boat propellers. He held out a hand, helped me onto the boat, where my sea legs sprang into immediate action.

"Where are we headed?" I asked.

"I'll give you one guess," the captain said.

"The ocean."

"Enggh." He made a buzzer sound then spoke in a deep, announcer's voice. "That is incorrect. We are going to the Gulf of Mexico and our destination is…?"

"Please say Cuba, please say Cuba…"

He lowered an eyebrow. "Do you have a visa?"

"Nope."

"Then we will *not* be visiting Cuba today! Jaxson, why don't you tell the nice lady what she's won?" He switched to a less annoying voice. "Today, Lily, you'll be visiting the Southernmost city in the U.S., Key West!"

"Yes." I pumped a fist. "How long does it take to get there?"

"Three and a half hours, same as driving from Miami, except a boat is so much nicer. I'll be doing the driving, and you…will be doing the relaxing."

"You know you had me at 'Boat…5 AM, right?" I grinned. Jax was doing a magnificent job of putting me in a positive frame of mind.

He extended a champagne glass at me. "Mimosa?"

"Impeccable service." I accepted the glass. "Thank you, Captain."

"My pleasure. Have a seat anywhere, Ms. Lily, and please…" He stepped behind the wheel and cranked on the engine. "Enjoy the ride."

I watched as he unwound the ropes and pushed us away from the dock, excited for our trip but also curious to know if this voyage would require an overnight stay or sharing of sleep facilities of any kind.

Whatever happens happens, I reminded myself.

We snuck through the waterway like gators' eyeballs cutting through the surface, stealthy and ready for adventure. I sat at the bow where I could see everything, from morning herons pecking the banks for fish to other boaters heading out to sea for early morning fishing. He lied, though. We did go out the Atlantic Ocean side for a few miles, so I could see the sun come up. For the first time in ages.

"That is gorgeous." I stared at the sunrise, its bright yellow rays radiating like on the box of Land O'Lakes butter.

Gradually, he turned the *Sea Witch* toward the gulf, ducking underneath the next highway bridge.

For the first hour, we were quiet. Jax could've used my captive audience to talk about himself, ask a zillion questions, or make small talk, but he didn't. Every so often, he pointed out a famous fishery or waterfront restaurant or the dorsal fin of a dolphin out for a morning swim, but that was it. I asked him to take a few photos of me to send Emily and Chase and not once did he ask to take a selfie with me. He focused on the ride, waved to other boaters, and offered me a banana, which I gladly accepted.

The quiet gave me time to think.

Luna really was a ghost, and Aunt Sylvie really was a cottage witch from the looks of it. I pulled the Tarot cards from my bag and sorted through them, thinking about the chaos in my life, how Chase wanted me home but also how I needed more time. I thought of Weasel hiring a friend of his girlfriend's but tried to push that out of my mind.

"So, why the *Sea Witch*?" I broke the silence.

"That's what my dad used to call my mom," he replied, eyes on the horizon.

"Was she?" I asked. "A sea witch?"

He gave a nod. "She loved the ocean and the beach. She spoke to the ocean. She'd go out there at night and just talk to it for hours, collect different samples of seawater depending on the ocean's mood."

"That's intriguing. What would she do with them?"

"Keep them around the house in little bottles, help people who came asking for help."

"Ah, so she offered services?"

He shook his head. "She never accepted money, but people would give her stuff anyway. They were always grateful to her for helping them."

"Sounds like she was pretty intuitive."

"She was."

I wasn't sure how bottles of seawater helped people, but as of yesterday, I wasn't sure how ghosts existed either. Or how statues could stare at people. Or how burning paper could release one of their burdens. If being in Skeleton Key had taught me anything, it was that I knew nothing.

"You don't have to talk about her. I was just curious about the name. I mean, unless you want to."

"She was a special lady."

It made me happy that he wanted to say more about her. "What was her name?"

"Aurelia," he said with a perfect Spanish accent. "Aurelia Gomez."

"Aurelia Gomez," I tried saying it in the same way. *Thank you for raising such a great son.*

"Have you ever been to Key West?" Jax asked.

"Never. Always meant to, but…" I couldn't really think of a reason except that I was always working, and that sounded so lame.

"You're a busy lady, Lily. Glad I got you on my boat."

"Me, too. Thank you for inviting me."

The morning was bright and cloudless when we arrived in Key West, and already things were bustling. The marina swelled with tourists boarding sailboats and schooners, the smell of seafood drifted in the air, and apparently, it was never too early for a drink.

"Not many rules here." Jax gestured to a young couple who walked by, beers in hand. He secured the ropes and helped me off the *Sea Witch* onto the wavering dock.

Seagulls swooped into the water for breakfast, and next to the dockside restaurant, a tall, shiny rooster proudly posed for photographs. So, this was Key West, the last depot before the Caribbean.

"I'm already loving this," I said.

We walked down the street, as Jax told me all about the island, how it was two miles wide and two and a half miles long, how the Spanish first named it Cayo Hueso, because it was covered in piles of bones when they arrived and nobody knew why. Apparently, the leading theory was that the Calusa Indians fled south and died here at the hands of the Spanish because there was nowhere left for them to run. "Hueso" sounded a bit like "west" to the English when they found the bones, hence they redubbed the island "Key West."

Today, the island was a collection of homes surrounded by lush vegetation, oceanside condos, marinas, restaurants up and down Duval Street, Mallory Square, where tourists gathered to watch the sun go down in the evening and to drink and party, a pirate museum, an Audubon House, the home of author Ernest Hemingway, and lots of other amazing places to visit.

Key West was rough around the edges, not quite polished and shiny like other Florida tourist towns. The first place we dove into, once the temperature started getting into the mid-90s, was the Treasure Hunter Museum.

"This place is cheesy, but I love it," Jax said. "Plus, there's something I'm dying to show you. I hope you haven't already seen it. Come on." He pulled me by the hand across the street before a scooter could run us down.

I made sure to purchase the entrance tickets before Jax could pull out his wallet. After all, he'd driven us here, and boat gas had to be quite expensive. Inside was dark, but once my eyesight adjusted, I loved looking at all the skeletons dressed as pirates, the Jolly Roger flags, and the mounds of fake gold on display. That was up front near the gift shop, but as we ventured further into the building, things got more interesting, and the gold got real.

Behind glass were numerous items found off the coasts, artifacts left in the depths by captured Spanish merchant ships, real doubloons, rusted anchors, cannonballs, weapons belonging to both the Spanish and the English. As always when I visited museums, I tried to imagine people 200-400 years ago using these items, sailing the seas, searching for riches, pillaging the land of those who already lived here. It was fascinating to remember that life was very different back then, though our footprints walked the same paths laid out by others before us.

"This is incredible." I stared at black-and-white photos of Key West before it was developed into the town it was today. Dirt roads led into jungle-like foliage, and wooden houses were erected by adventuresome, brave pioneers, posing with tired, vacant eyes and thin, linen clothing.

"And we think we have it rough today," I said.

Jax nodded. "Yep. Imagine living out here when there was nothing? Come, follow me."

I knew he was leading me toward whatever he wanted to show me. When we arrived at a wall covered in more photos, I wasn't sure what I was looking at.

Rumrunners of the Upper Keys, the display sign read. Across a map of the island chain were more black-and-white photos depicting the development of the islands through the 19th and 20th centuries, all the old homes, some of which were destroyed by hurricanes over the years.

"Are you looking closely?" Jax asked.

"What am I looking for?" I peered beyond the glass enclosure.

"You'll know it when you see it."

Finally, my gaze raked across a photo I'd already noticed, except this time I spotted something I hadn't caught before. It was a house—my house. Aunt Sylvie's house. That was the same porch, those were the same windows, and right there, to the left…

"Wait…is that?" I gasped.

"Yep, the same garden. It's that old. This is Rumrunning Annie's house."

"I knew it belonged to her once—Sid told me—but wow, she's got a spot in this museum?"

"Yep, see there? It says how she used to make rum and whiskey on the property during Prohibition days, but the front of the house where the kitchen is became a bakery. That way, when police or Coast Guard came sniffing, they thought all she was selling were pies."

"Key lime pies."

"Fun, huh?"

"Sneaky lady."

"Amazing lady," Captain Jax said. "The distillery was her bread and butter, so when Prohibition put a monkey wrench in her business, she found ways to keep going. So did other women of Skeleton Key. Other houses were a burlesque theater, a bordello, a Cuban cigar factory…"

"All women-owned?"

"All women-owned. All unmarried, separated, or divorced, which was pretty risqué in those days. Although…Annie Jackson *may* have had a little companionship." He pointed to another photo off to the right.

I felt my face go cold when I realized that the tiny smudge in the corner of the photo marked 1931, looking through ninety years of time with her bright eyes, was... "Luna?"

Jax smiled, pleased with himself. "Didn't think you'd see that, did you?"

"But it can't be. I mean, it looks like her, but..."

He laughed. "Get used to it, Lily. Skeleton Key is haunted."

"No shit." I stared at the photos in complete and utter awe. That was definitely Aunt Sylvie's house, mostly unchanged, except there was no fence surrounding the yard back then, way more key lime trees, and one could see clearly to the beach from the front yard.

But Luna? The old Lily would've insisted it was just a look-alike, but the new Lily knew—knew in my heart it was her.

I felt a deep sense of pride well up inside of me. Suddenly, the amount of time I'd spent putting into the house to fix it up didn't feel so extraneous. I was happy to help Annie renovate her old home and wondered if maybe she was still there, too. Had Annie opened my window to let in the breezes? Left me a hat to help work on her yard? Called me out to the beach to help me sort out my life?

"Wait, did you say Annie Jackson?" I raised an eyebrow.

"Yep. I'm named after her. My dad's family has lived on the island since those days, and he says we're related to her. Skeleton Key is in our blood."

"So's rumrunning. Jax, you're descended from pirates. Argh!"

He laughed. "Not quite. Annie was good people. Just a woman who got by during hard times."

"I love it." Annie understood me. Reassuring to know a kickass woman like her was watching out for me.

And yet, Jax thought about selling his house to a cruise line. I didn't want to say anything but knowing the history of the street we lived on would've changed my mind. He must've needed the money pretty bad.

"Is there a state organization, like a historical society, that can declare the island an historic site? I mean, there's enough history here to warrant protecting it," I said.

Jax shrugged. "There is, but all we have left are photos. The houses have changed too much. It's not like we've preserved the integrity of the original structures. There's really nothing left to show."

"Ah."

"It's not like other towns where gold is found off the coast, or pirates left behind their ships—tangible things that can be displayed. Most of the homes are in bad shape. Face it—at some point, Skeleton Key will fade into history."

That was a terrible thought. Here, Key West retained its charm, whereas Skeleton Key risked getting turned into a tourist trap. I wondered if more of the homes' original splendor was restored, if the neighborhood might be eligible to be nominated as an official, historic part of the Keys.

"No whiskey bottles or distillery left?" I asked, and Jax shook his head. "Too bad. It would've been cool to visit a real Prohibition-era house containing real rumrunning items."

"Tell me about it, but all that stuff was seized by the government. Any and all liquor found during the final raids were probably kept for themselves. You know how that is." He mimicked drinking down a bottle of rum, complete with hiccup. "Anyway, that's what I wanted you to see."

"Thank you so much. This was really a treat."

"Now that we got the educational stuff out of the way, let's go have fun. First stop, Hemingway House. Then whatever you want to do after that."

"Can we duck into a few bars and get sloshed?" I asked, surprised by my own question. After the day I had yesterday, I felt ready for anything. Unabashedly adventurous. I was having—fun. Actual fun.

"I like the way you think. Come on, girl." He tugged me by the hand. I didn't complain.

We spent the day visiting sites, taking photos with six-toed cats at the Hemingway House, and visiting a beautiful butterfly conservatory. We took the obligatory photo by the Southernmost Point buoy and sampled homemade coconut and mango ice cream at a creamery. When the day was at its most boiling, we ducked into a seedy bar and ordered shots of local rum and beer.

Good thing Jax was a good, solid body to lean on. I must've held onto his arm for hours to keep from falling on my butt.

"Bartender? I need a crane to lift this dead weight off my arm." The way Jax said it set me giggling for ten minutes straight.

After that, we laughed over the dumbest things and watched a group of young over-21 kids barely hold their liquor. "Amateurs," I said. "Not us, though. We're veterans. We've been though war and shit."

"That's right. We've been dumped, lied to, burned, turned into Swiss cheese, and lived to tell the tale." Jax pressed his forehead into mine. "And we're sexier because of it."

"Yeah, life battle scars are sexy. They build character."

"Yeah."

"Yeah. Hey, is it me or is this place clearing out?" I noticed people leaving by the dozens.

Jax checked the time on his phone. "It's nearly sunset. Everyone's heading outside. Let's go."

"Already? How did the day go by so fast?"

"We were having fun. Come on. Take your beer."

Snatching my bottle, I walked into the street where the sky had turned a rich coral hue, and purple clouds mottled the evening sky, as we crossed street after street to get to Mallory Square. We found the perfect little spot away from the crowds to watch the sun descend over the water. There was music and laughter in the air, the perfect end to a perfect day.

"Cheers." I clinked my bottle against Jax's. "To Rumrunning Annie."

"To Annie. And Sylvie. And Lily," he replied. "And all the amazing women who've turned that house into magic."

Turned that house into magic. Was that what I was doing? "You've helped, too, you know."

He nodded in acknowledgement.

I didn't correct him by saying I'd never technically lived there. I was only a visitor, passing through. But it felt nice being included in that list, and for a couple more weeks, I could continue to pretend. Evade reality a little longer. I might even bring myself to believe my divorce was over, because, maybe it was all the rum and beer, I really wanted to get closer to Jax, now that my inhibitors and overly-rational thinking were long gone.

The sun went down, crowds cheered, and people resumed their partying. Just another day in paradise.

GABRIELLE KEYES

"You want to go home?" Jax asked. "Or do we want to hang on the boat for a while longer?" A tone of something deep and raw in his voice told me we were headed into unfamiliar waters. Unlike the other night, I wasn't afraid this time. I wanted to draw him close to me, take comfort and friendship from him in any way possible.

Setting down my bottle, I reached up toward his shoulders. His eyes held mine for a hazy, fog-filled moment. Without hesitation, he read me expertly and dipped his face toward mine. His lips tasted like the sun, tongue like rum and coconut, and skin smelled like the salty sea. Yes, I wanted to hang at the boat for a while, and though that might've been the alcohol talking, I didn't care.

The real me wanted to feel good again.

The real me deserved it.

He pulled back, ran his thumb across my chin. "That answers my question."

15

If the Sea Witch is a-rockin', don't come a-knockin'.

I must've thought that several times on our way back to the boat, so by the time we returned to the marina, and Captain Jax set the vessel out to open water, I was agonizing pretty hard about what to do.

On one hand, I wanted his closeness. I missed intimacy, and Jax was the perfect friend with benefits, if you know what I mean, wink, wink. On the other, I wanted to wait and do things right. Stay away from men for a while. This is Me Time. Yadda, yadda.

But why impose rules on myself? All my life I'd lived by rules—fall in love, get married in your twenties, have a big wedding, do successful things together, make two or more babies—and as Chase so eloquently said, I still got shafted. Rules had gotten me into this mess in the first place. Instead of living by rules, maybe it was time to try living by instinct.

Follow my gut more.

Listen to my intuition.

I was lying on the bow, staring up at the stars when Jax, done with taking us out to open water, lay beside me, propped up on an elbow. "I can see your wheels turning. Changed your mind yet?"

"Would it be okay if I did? I'm in a really indecisive state."

"Of course." He got comfortable next to me. "I've been where you are. I get it. Anything you want is fine. I'm just happy I got to come down to the Conch Republic not by myself, for once." He flipped onto his back and stared up at the stars with me. "You've been fun to hang out with. Far as I'm concerned, it's already a perfect day."

Same, but that distrustful little voice in my head that felt men were natural born liars kept niggling at me. He was probably saying that to get me into bed.

So what? It was me, my own voice, a new side of me. *This is about you. What do* you *want?*

Hell, for now, I just wanted to kiss. That's what I wanted, and if it progressed from there, I'd worry about that later. There—decision made.

And kiss, we did.

I rolled toward him, pulling him into my orbit, and we connected, effortlessly, like I'd known him forever. It was nice kissing Jax. He was good at understanding what I wanted without my having to speak it aloud. I was never a vocal seductress. Some women took the guesswork out of sex by telling their partners everything they wanted, but I was always different. I much preferred for a man to read my body than be told what to do. Made them more men than boys in my eyes.

And with kisses like his, things got intense pretty quickly. Our hands headed places I hadn't thought I'd be by the end of the day, and suddenly my brain reminded me how hard and fast I'd fallen in the past. Better to take things slow.

I pulled away, smiling, nervous energy making me giggle. Jax matched that energy and yelled, "Hoo! Two cold showers, STAT." His arms splayed out flat, and I loved the way his wide chest heaved up and down as he caught his breath.

I'd done that to him—me.

"No kidding." I closed my eyes, let the boat rock me into a dizzying spell. "Jax..."

"Yep?"

"If you could have a fresh start at life," I said, hooking my pinky through his. "What would you do differently?"

"I would be a much more chill baby. Not throw my Cheerios around so much."

"No," I snort-laughed. "I mean, later on. Fast forward to your twenties, let's say. Would you do everything the same, or what?"

He ran a hand through his hair. "I've thought about this a lot. I can't say I would stay away from Annette, because that would mean I wouldn't have my son, and I was meant to be his dad."

"Fair enough." I tried to imagine Jax as a father. I bet he was a really good one.

"Things may not be perfect right now, but I'll see him again soon. We'll start a new kind of relationship. The old one is gone. I just have to accept that."

Relationships with kids shifted. We no longer were heroes in their eyes. If we did things right, we shifted into a new kind of friendship.

"Anything else?" I asked.

"I would change the way I reacted to certain things in the past. I spent a lot of time fighting the tide, trying to change Annette's mind, getting pissed at stuff I couldn't control. None of it served me in the end. It only made me bitter, and bitter wasn't who I was."

"So, you feel like you wasted too much time on the negative."

"For sure, but more on stuff I couldn't change."

"Yeah, same here. It took me a year."

"For what?" Jax asked.

"To throw Derek's shit onto the street and set it on fire. A year. I'm angry it took me so long. And angry at Derek, for putting me in that situation."

"Hey, you had to go through it. Feel all your feelings."

"I guess."

"We all process trauma differently. Because you know it's trauma you went through, right?" He turned to me. "Real PTSD. Divorce is no joke."

"I know, but the world makes you feel like you should get over it quickly. Like, how is anyone supposed to let go so fast after someone you loved does you harm?"

"True."

"No one talks about the sadness that comes with it, the crushed dreams, the ideals of perfection, the security that got stomped on, the way I feel like a failure."

"Hey, no, no, hold on." He took my hand and slid his fingers through mine. "You are *not* a failure. Your ex is the failure. What kind of dude gives up on someone like you? The kind who doesn't feel he deserves you and knew it deep down inside. I can tell you that much."

I shook my head. "You're too nice."

"I'm dead serious is what I am. You are, holy crap, you are one of the most successful, talented, smart, amazing, funny, friendly, caring, um, freakin' gorgeous women I know. How the hell did I get you on my boat?"

I giggled. "You threw my phone on the beach."

"Is that what I did?"

"Yep. Nobody's ever had the nerve to do anything like that to me before. People always do what I say. I'm the boss. But I needed the reminder. I needed to disengage from his bullshit. So, thank you."

"What about you? Is there anything you would do differently?" he asked.

"Hmm…" I'd wanted him to answer first for a reason. Because I didn't know. "I think maybe I would've done more stuff for me. For a long time, I made decisions based on what was right for Derek, since he was the face of our outfit."

"An ugly face, I'm just sayin'."

I laughed. "He's not ugly."

"No? He looks like he got whacked with a broomstick. Twice."

"Jax! We can't all be naturally rugged boat captains, who for all intents and purposes, should be attracting legions of sexy women onto his vessel."

"I guess I only attract the good ones."

I squeezed his hand. I could've used Jax to make me feel good about myself the whole last year. "Thanks. So, yeah, there were trips I wanted to take, things I wanted to do, that I set aside all so his celebrity ass could have the spotlight."

"Women sacrifice themselves all the time. I watched my mother do it. Luckily, toward the end of their lives, she got more of a say on what she wanted, as my dad gave up the spotlight."

"That's nice, I guess."

"Sort of. It meant she went on trips by herself, took painting lessons by herself, made pottery by herself."

"Aww, that's sad. I'm sorry."

"Don't be. She was happy. They found a way to still be together by being apart, I guess. I'm just glad she got around to doing those things, because soon after, they couldn't do much anymore."

"I guess the moral of the story is to take advantage of life while we still can," I sighed so deeply, I was sure it could be heard all the way home.

"It's what I'm trying to do," Jax agreed. "Just want to do more, you know? I want to feel like I'm a part of something important, not just floating through life like a piece of driftwood."

"I hear you," I said.

I did. "I feel like I've worked enough to leave a worthwhile legacy for my children, but now I want to work less, or work smarter."

"I get that, but not to the point where you forget to have fun." He tapped my nose. "Can I tell you something? It's kind of hard for me to say."

"Of course."

"When you were yelling on the phone with your ex, I heard it—the rage. I've been there. It makes you crazy. Divorce will make you feel like there's a madman living inside you."

I sighed. "I know. I'm trying to change that."

"You will. But every time I talked to you before that, you sounded so chill, it kind of caught me by surprise. That's why I snatched your phone away. Still, I'm sorry. I shouldn't have done that."

"It's okay. You're a good man, Jax. And may I say thank you—so much—for inviting me to Key West. I really, really needed this."

"I didn't invite you. I ordered you." He winked, a naughty smile on his lips. "I could see, at that moment, what you needed. A good friend can do that, I think. And you showed up, because you trusted me. So, thank *you*." He kissed me again, but this time, short and sweet. I appreciated something about that so much.

"Should we get going?" I asked. "It's a three-hour trip. Not that I want to, mind you. I haven't seen this many stars since the *Cooking Network's Christmas Special*. But those stars were snotty food snobs."

Jax's quiet laughter sounded like sniffles. I loved that we were having a great time, but I really did want to get back now, while I had my life in focus. "Aye, aye, Captain."

"Sorry, didn't mean to be bossy toward the boss."

"You're not. It's just you're the captain now. Come, take the wheel." He scrambled to his feet and held out his hand.

"Wait, you're going to let me drive? I've never driven a boat before."

He helped me to my feet. "And I've never let anyone drive my boat before. Hurry, boss lady, before I change my mind."

16

With the downstairs painted, the new furniture in, the kitchen cabinets bright, and the garden looking spiffier, Aunt Sylvie's house sat a little taller today. Sure, the outside still needed work, but Jax had put in the new lantern and sections of floorboard on the porch, and in just three weeks, the value had probably shot up.

I found I kept walking out to the front yard to stare at the house. I kept matching the way it looked now with the way it looked in Annie's time in my head. Luna hadn't come around in the three days since I'd gone to Key West and seen her in a photo dated 1931, but knowing her, she'd show up at the strangest times. Getting back from a shell shop on Overseas Highway, I pulled out the front door key but once again found the door ajar.

"Hello?" I called.

Nobody answered. Of course, nobody answered. That door just liked to pop open whenever it felt like it. Bowie came to the door but kept his distance. I was always amazed he never escaped, as though an invisible forcefield kept him in place.

I imagined Annie, still here, still watching over her house, maybe opening doors and windows, forgetting that she was no longer alive.

I was about to enter when I noticed a paper package off to the right on the kitchen windowsill. I unfolded it and saw a small yellowtail inside with a note:

Missed my best customer. On me. – S.
PS. Didn't leave this on the back porch.
Wanted to make sure you saw it.

Dang, I missed Sid, and I was looking forward to hearing his take on Luna, Sylvie's witchy items, and maybe even Jax. Figured he could give me his honest opinion since according to him, men these days weren't to be trusted. "Thanks for the fish," I said, stepping inside.

Something was different. I couldn't place my finger on exactly what it was. The new furniture was giving the house a more chill vibe, but I was pretty sure it had nothing to do with that.

"Bo, did you change something?" I sat cross-legged on the floor to hug the white beast. He purred in my lap and pushed his head into my hand.

"What's that, you say? You see Annie when I'm not around? She takes care of this house and all those who live in it?" I chuckled, but holy heck, where did that thought come from?

Finally, I realized what it was. In the corner of the dining room, where the tall armoire filled with Sylvie's plastic fish dinnerware usually sat, the piece was moved to the side about eight to ten inches, exposing a two-foot by two-foot sliding door in the wall. I got up to peer at it, realizing for the first time ever that the armoire sat on caster wheels.

"Who moved this?" I looked at Bowie.

Why I kept expecting my cat to answer was beyond me, and why I hadn't just run out of the house screaming was even weirder.

"Did you move that, Annie?"

Leaning my head on the dusty carpet, I slid the door aside and looked inside the wall. It wasn't so much a hiding spot as a mini closet, filled with a bunch of my aunt's things. Photo albums—I pulled out four. Journals—two, fat ones. A sketchbook and several Cuban cigar boxes.

I sat cross-legged, as Bowie rubbed his shedding body all over me. "What do we have here?"

Photos of Aunt Sylvie in her younger days. Look at that Coppertone glowing skin and curvy body, posing in a bikini on the beach like a mermaid on the sand. In others, she danced with her friends, twirling sparklers through the night air. Big smiles. A man, a woman. The man looked a lot like Jax.

Where those his parents?

Handkerchiefs. Bouffant hair on one of the other two beach babes, who looked like teens. One had a boyfriend. Thick, black sunglasses. A sexy young man in another photo with her, his arm around her shoulders, kissing her cheek in one, smiling big in another.

I flipped the photo over. *1979. Love this chick. – Sid.*

Heyyy. Salty Sid really did know my aunt back in the day? They were friends, maybe more by the look of that kiss. How cool was that? He was pretty darn handsome back in the day. "Nice catch, Sylvie. I approve."

Flipping through photos made me sad about the way time passes. Like the ocean eroding a bit of your youth each time it creeps onto the sand. The journals were even harder to look at. So much of Sylvie's writings had to do with nature, the ocean, the sun, stars, her friends, the magic they made, the friendships forged and lost.

For a woman who never married, she lived quite a bit. In fact, what a dumb thing to think. It was because she'd never married that she lived as much as she had. And now, she sat surrounded by four walls and a roof in Tampa, cared for by nurses, wasting away. I had to take these things to her. I had to show them to her and make her happy again for just one day. Maybe I could convince her to come home. Maybe Mom and I could pay for a live-in nurse.

In her sketchbook, Sylvie had quite a collection of drawings. Something called The Wheel of the Year, divided into twelve sections. Litha, Yule, Ostara, Samhain, another name for Halloween. For each season, she listed herbs, crystals, oils, flowers, incense, colors, all accompanied by drawings of candles, crowns, blooms, constellations. The pentagram was a motif in her sketches, yet nothing looked evil to me.

Air, fire, water, earth, surrounded by spirit, she wrote underneath one of them.

So many symbols. *The divine feminine,* she wrote here. *The power of the goddess,* she wrote there. Was Sylvie really into all this metaphysical stuff? I had no idea, but now I knew her in an entirely new light. On another page, she'd drawn a house—this house. Her house. Annie's house. All around were vines, hibiscus, frangipani, and the sun above, shining its loving rays on a happy little cottage.

A cottage witch.

I flipped through her photos one more time, trying to find my mother in any of them, but didn't see her. We didn't visit Aunt Sylvie but once a year for one week during summer vacation, and Mom never talked about her much, except to roll her eyes and say that her sister who lived in Florida was so odd. To be honest, I now felt resentful for that. Had Mom and Dad purposely kept me and Gary away from Aunt Sylvie all because she was a little strange?

The more I examined the photos, the more I realized one of the beach babes must be Heloise. She'd mentioned being married once, so if I was right, that guy in the photo was once her husband. In the albums showing the earliest days, I didn't see Jeanine, but in later ones from the 90s or 00s, I definitely did. There she was with funny bangs and a cigarette, shooting a bird at the camera.

Many photos were missing or had fallen out.

Sylvie's life had been magical, and now it was nearly over. I sat with albums and journals scattered around me and wondered where I'd go from here two weeks from now. Would I return to NYC to get reabsorbed by the restaurant business, or would I go and twirl sparklers in the air, for once? Join in the circle dance. Boat to Key West. Pet manatees.

There was wonder here in the Keys. Granted, there was wonder to be found everywhere, but Skeleton Key was full of it, and it took a few new people to show me that. The magic hadn't come from new gray paint or Instagrammable new cushions. It'd come from friendships, something I'd severely lacked.

The drawing after the house was a closeup where Sylvie had drawn a sign hanging from a lantern. *Sylvie's Bed & Breakfast,* the sign read.

"No way, Aunt Syl. I didn't know you dreamed of opening a bed and breakfast one day, same as me!" That did it. Now I *had* to visit her. I'd have to call my mother.

"Siri, call Mom." I grabbed the journals and placed it all on top of the glass dining table.

"Calling Mom 'Killjoy' Autumn."

"Hello? Lily, is that you?"

"Yes, Mom. Don't you see my name on your phone? You should have it programmed to say Lily or Lil or daughter, at the very least."

"It says Potential Spam. Does that seem right?"

"No. I'll fix that later. Hey, I'm sitting here surrounded by a bunch of things of Sylvie's that I found in a hidden closet."

"Uh-oh. Are they bottles with funny little sayings on them like 'mugwort,' 'sleeping oil,' 'attraction oil,' and the like? Such nonsense."

"No." But now I had to find those. "Most are pictures through the years, but many are drawings. I had no idea she was so heavily into astrology, new age-y stuff, Mom. You never told me that." I flipped to a page filled with chants for various reasons—to clear stagnant air, to rid the home of negative energy, to harness sexual magic.

Whoa, Nelly.

"It's all nonsense, Lily. Why she spent so much time studying something without any basis in science is beyond me, but we all have our quirks, I suppose."

"Maybe it's not based in science...yet," I stressed. "Either way, now I feel like I never got to know her. I would've loved talking with her more, but for some reason, I got the impression she was a freak, or mentally ill, or I don't know what."

"Well, I didn't know you were into it either, or I would've suggested you talk to her."

"I—I might've asked more questions."

154

"Are you blaming me for your lack of kinship with your aunt, Lily? I suppose I could've talked about her more, but she never made an effort to come visit either. That house in Skeleton Key was her little bubble."

"You mean her whole world?" I could understand why. It was a self-sustainable ecosystem, an easy one to lose herself within. I'd only been here three weeks—Sylvie, a lifetime.

"I'm not blaming you. I'm just saying I would've liked to know more about her. Anyway, the reason I'm calling is because I want to go see her. Maybe bring her some of these things. Is her address still the same? It's the one in Tampa, right?"

A flicker of silence.

"Mom?"

"Yes, I'm here. Honey, go if you must, but Aunt Sylvie is not the same."

"What do you mean?"

"She's…well, her mind is long gone. I didn't want to tell you. I haven't wanted to talk about it, to be honest." My mother's voice cracked. In her hesitation, I felt a wave of suppressed pain emanating through the line. "She won't recognize you, honey. She won't even know your name. She didn't know mine last time I spoke with her."

"I knew it was bad, but not that bad. Is it Alzheimer's?" I sat at the dining chair, running my fingers over the leather-bound journals.

"We thought she had the typical dementia of many her age," Mom said, as though she wasn't older than Aunt Sylvie. "But over the last year, it's gotten worse. Much worse."

"Yet, she asked me to come check on her house. It can't be that bad if she remembers she has a house and a niece who might look at it for her."

"Honey. I'm the one who asked you to go check the house for her. The cruise line wanted a response from Aunt Sylvie, and since I've been handling her affairs, I sent you, since I thought you could use a week or two vacation anyway. I didn't know you'd be there nearly a month, and I certainly didn't think you'd be interested in Aunt Sylvie's…interests."

"Seriously?" My mouth gaped open.

"Was I wrong to send you? It does seem like you've been having a nice time, from the photos you've been posting."

"No, it's been great. I just…please…next time know that you can tell me the truth. I'm tired of lies. You must understand that, don't you?" I held my voice in check, but I was perturbed my mother felt she had to deceive me.

"Yes, honey. I'm sorry. That was wrong of me."

In my seat, I shifted and dropped my forehead to the glass. "It's fine…fine. I haven't been totally honest either. Look, I've been fixing things for Sylvie in the event she decided to rent or sell."

"Like what?"

"Like painting, and fixing the porch, sprucing up the garden…"

So beautiful, the mystery voice whispered. Quickly, I scanned around for Luna but didn't see her.

"Best not to waste any more money, dear. Let it sell As Is when it comes to that."

"But I didn't know she wasn't cognizant," I said, still looking for Luna, "that she wouldn't love pics of the place when I was done with it. I feel terrible that so many of her treasured belongings are here. Why didn't she take them when she left?"

"Lily, she took very little. As for things you found, Sylvie always hid things. Even as a child, I can attest to her hiding strange objects from your grandparents all the time."

"She probably felt judged," I said, annoyed. Living one's truth wasn't a big thing back in the day.

"You can have them," Mom said. "It's the only way you'll get to know her at this point."

That was an incredibly sad thing to hear. Seemed I'd lost my chance to really know Aunt Sylvie. "How long does she have?" I asked.

"No clue." Mom sighed. I heard a sniffle when she rarely cried. "Go and see her if it'll make you feel better. I'll send you the address. But if I were you, I'd stay and remember her exactly the way you saw her in those photo albums. It's better this way, dear. Trust me."

After she hung up, I sat at the dining room table a long time, wondering what is life. Why were we even here? Why be given amazing chances to create, build memories, laugh, love, lose and love again, only to end in such a tragic way? Aunt Sylvie should be dying here at home, surrounded by beloved friends, not in an assisted living facility with strangers. With Heloise making her exquisite dinners, Jeanine cracking crude jokes, Salty Sid bringing her yellowtail. Jax fixing up her yard.

Yes, she'd had a good life, from the looks of it, but it still wasn't fair. Here one day, carted off the next.

Something from inside the wall reflected the dining room light. I crouched again to grab it—a piece of wood about two feet long, eight inches tall, painted glossy white, pencil sketch of letters in a curly font. *Sylvie's Bed &*

Breakfast, the sign read, the same sign she'd sketched in her book. At some point, she'd intended to open her home to guests, and what a wonderful location for a bed-and-breakfast this would've made.

But life took over, she never got the chance.

A dream unfinished. Unfulfilled.

Now she never would.

17

Bowie and I sat on the back porch for most of the next few days while I pored over Sylvie's journals, and guess what? Sex magic had nothing to do with blood and evil, like I thought it had, for some stupid reason. Simply put, it's about envisioning something you really, really want and imagining yourself receiving it while *at the same time having an orgasm.*

As in, YES, YES, YES, FINALLY, A MILLION DOLLARS! while gripping the sheets in ecstasy. Your brain believes it is ecstatic because of *the thing*, so eventually, you do receive *the thing*. I resolved to try this out sometime just to see if it worked, but today, I was waiting for a buyer to come pick up Sylvie's old furniture. I'd managed to sell it for $250 for the whole set.

The distant chime of Salty Sid's bell wafted in on the breeze just as I was about to go inside, however, so I stood on the beach, waving him down.

"Ahoy, Lily of the Lilliputians!"

"Ahoy, Sid of the Symphonic Seas!" I waved.

"Where does that name come from?" he called.

"I do not know!" I called back. He laughed.

When Sid arrived on my stretch of beach, he pulled his boat onto the sand and jumped out carrying a medium-sized box filled with what looked like tons of mail.

"What's this?"

"Something I've had for some time now." He lifted his *Get Leid* cap off his head and scratched his balding head. "When Sylvie's mailbox started overflowing after she left, I started coming by to collect it for her. It's all unopened, you can see. I would never be dishonest by her."

"I never thought that for a minute, Sid. Thank you for bringing this." I sifted through the envelopes—insurance bills, power bills, coupon booklets, hospital bills, a message from the local representative…junk.

"Ah, it's the least I could do, Miss Lily. You know, your aunt and I had some truly fun times. She was a joy to hang out with."

"I found photos in an album, and I believe I recognized one particularly handsome fella in a few." I winked at him, and Salty Sid actually blushed.

"Oh, heh, heh, yeah, I was a looker."

I laughed. "If you do say so yourself?"

"Yep. I'm only sorry I never got to say goodbye." He looked off toward the horizon.

I could feel the sadness emanating off him.

"I'm so sorry." I spread two envelopes into a fan and blocked the sun with them. "I'll gladly pass on the message that you say hello next time I see her. Although…" I thought back to what my mother said about her sister's declining health. "She probably won't remember anyone, Sid, I'm sorry to say. She's not doing well."

He nodded. "I figured. Did you get the yellowtail I left ya?" he asked, obviously avoiding the topic.

"I sure did. Let me send you money for it, please."

"No need. It's on me. You've given me a reason to stop at this house again. I missed coming round here." He picked up the box and carried it to my back porch, dropping it off inside. "Anyway, I may see you later. I heard the Atlantis Cruise Line rep is stopping by today."

"Is he?"

"Yep, and I'm curious to hear what they have to offer this time. It's always something new, though I think this may be their last visit. Catch ya later, alligator!" He jumped back into his boat and gave me a thumb's up.

"After a while, crocodile."

I was loading Aunt Sylvie's old furniture in the back of some dude named Jesus's pickup truck when the sound of flip-flops flapping on gravel came rushing towards me.

"Pulitzer!" Jeanine darted across our properties.

"Thanks," I said to the guy handing me $250 cash for the whole rattan set. Not bad for garbage. He started backing out, nearly clipping Jeanine in the process.

"Careful, most accidents happen a mile from home." I smirked at the guy. "What's up, Jeanini Panini. See? Two can play that game."

"Has he been here yet?" She doubled over to catch her breath.

"Who?"

"The cruise line rep. Their attorney. He's here. He's on the island. He's been making the rounds with his BMW and his fancy-pants slacks. I think he's still over on Coconut Court." She turned toward the house.

"Wait. What is he doing? Checking in with residents?"

"Harassing. I'm going to call the police," Jeanine said.

"On what grounds?" I laughed.

"Treachery," she replied. "I'll call you when I see him, so you can come over. Safety in numbers, Pulitzer!"

Shaking my head, I looked at Sylvie's little Victorian cottage. The paint and few repairs had done it a world of good, but was it worth keeping? Property value in the Keys had skyrocketed lately, Jax told me, so Atlantis Cruise Line might not be able to offer what they could each get with a private buyer.

"Sylvie...what would you do?" I whispered. "Is it time to move on?"

At that moment, I spotted a shiny light blue BMW turning into Key Lime Lane. "He's here," I murmured, then louder so Jeanine, Heloise, and Jax might hear me. "He's here!"

The BMW parked in an empty lot at the street entrance, as if he knew he wasn't welcome to come any closer. Out stepped a man in perfectly pressed slacks, a gleaming watch, and a white guayabera, complete with cigar in the upper left pocket.

He waved. I twiddled my fingers and headed for Jeanine's house, texting Jax at the same time. Whatever this man had to say, he could say it to all of us at once. Heloise was already at the door, looking forlorn like a lost puppy.

"Ugh, I guess we're doing this," she said aloud.

"He's only a rep, guys. Let's hear what he has to say. Remember, nobody has the right to take anything of yours without your permission." I glanced over to see Jax stepping out of his house in shorts, flip-flops, and nothing else. *Good Lord, man, put those perfect pecs away.*

The lawyer approached the waist-high picket fence carrying manila packets under his arm. "Good afternoon, folks. Yes, it's me again. I know how thrilled you are."

Jax opened the gate for him. "After you."

"Thank you, sir. I don't think we've met," he said, extending his hand to me the moment he saw me. "I'm Favor Wallace from Atlantis Cruise Line, and you are?"

"Lily Blanchett, niece of Sylvia Collier." I shook his hand.

"Right, I believe I've been in communication with your mother. Are Ms. Mabry and Ms. Bryant here?" he asked. I assumed he meant Heloise and Jeanine. Heloise stepped outside with her paper fan. "Ah, there's Ms. Mabry. And Ms. Bryant? Getting her shotgun, I trust?"

I withheld a smile. I knew how much Jeanine didn't like the guy, but so far, he seemed fine to me. It must've been difficult having his job.

"I think we're all here," Heloise said. "Except for Sid, but you probably got to him already."

"I have not," he replied.

"He was just here not thirty minutes ago," I said.

"I'll go get him. Start without me." Jax ran off in the direction of the beach.

"Would it be better if we sat inside, away from the boiling sun?" Mr. Wallace wiped a line of sweat on his hairline, clearly hoping for an invitation indoors.

"You can start." Jeanine emerged from the house, lit a cigarette, and took her seat on the shady porch rocking chair.

"Alrighty, then. I'll cut right to the chase." Mr. Wallace stacked his packets on the railing and accidentally knocked over one of Heloise's garden gnomes with his loafer. "Oops. My bad." He tried fixing it, but the garden gnome and his magical mushroom would only lean. "I don't know if you've kept abreast of the market, but your property's gone up in value."

"Of course, it has," Jeanine mumbled.

"Jeanine." I shot her a look. "Let the man speak."

She rolled her eyes and blew out smoke.

"Now that working remote has become a more viable option in this post-pandemic world, many out-of-towners are moving from places like New York and Los Angeles, where they no longer need to work in the city, in droves to South Florida, many to the Keys, looking for homes that match what they were paying in mortgage or rent before."

"Wow, island homes cheaper than an apartment in the City." I shook my head. "So, it's come to this."

"Yeah, well, I'd rather sell to private buyers than to you guys," Jeanine interrupted. "They'd keep the integrity of the house pretty much the same."

"You think?" Mr. Wallace said. "Don't think they won't gut it and refurbish from the ground up, but selling to them is entirely your prerogative, Ms. Bryant." Classy Mr. Wallace pulled a handkerchief from his pocket and dabbed his forehead.

I gestured for him to move closer to the shade. Jeanine gave me a look. "If you wait a second, I see Jax and Sid coming back." I pointed across the property at the men heading our way.

Mr. Wallace saluted Sid. "Ah, the resident pirate. Welcome back, Mr. Roberts."

"Pirates are dirty, raping scoundrels who don't deserve glorification. Don't compare me to them ever again." Sid crossed his arms, showing off his anchor tattoo.

"Fair enough, Mr. Roberts. My apologies. Anyhoo…" He repeated what he'd said so far, adding, "Your properties are going for anywhere from $2M to $2.5M in some of your cases." He looked at me. "But we're prepared to offer you a package with benefits that we hope will please you."

"Spill the beans, Slacks. I've got fritters in the oil." Jeanine blew smoke in his direction.

"Our offer is $1.75M for the canal property," he said, looking at Jax. "$1.5M for this one, and $2M for Ms. Collier's."

"I thought you said we'd be pleased," Heloise said, fanning her neck.

"Also," Mr. Wallace went on, "your choice of unit in the beachfront condo we'll be building, each of which is worth at least $1.5M. No fees for life. Free amenities—gym, pool, cabanas, etc. Plus…use of recreation facilities—water park, private beach, tiki bar."

"We don't want your dumb condo." It was Salty Sid, being salty. He shot Mr. Wallace a bird, complete with SpongeBob bandage on his finger.

"Right on, Roberts!" Jeanine gave Sid an air high-five.

"I feel the love emanating from you all, and believe me when I say how grateful I am to you for that." Mr. Wallace picked up the packets and passed them around. "But there's more. Atlantis Cruise Line is also prepared to offer free cruises…for life. Any of our eight ships, on any of our voyages throughout the Caribbean."

That got Jeanine and Heloise to glance at each other without comment, and even Salty Sid remained quiet. Jax and I exchanged glances.

Mr. Wallace knew he'd just gained a half-step in approval ratings. "So, to summarize, you still get to live on

Skeleton Key, only it will be called Cabana Cay, you get to live in a brand-new beachfront condo, completely paid for, and you get to use pretty much anything on the island, any time. Can I get an A-men?" Wallace laughed, but no one laughed with him.

He cleared his throat.

Silence as everyone eyed each other.

"In other words, you are our premier guests for the rest of your natural lives. The package doesn't provide provisions for the spirit world, however." Mr. Wallace laughed awkwardly, tapped Heloise's rainbow ornament above his head.

"It should. Where are our resident ghosts supposed to go?" Salty Sid asked. It did not help our case that his hat still said *Get Leid*.

Mr. Wallace thought this to be funny and shook his head in more amazement at my neighbors. "Ah, you guys kill me. Any questions?"

"I was serious," Sid said. "You'll have yourself one haunted condo, you will."

"It's a risk the cruise line is willing to accept, Mr. Roberts," Mr. Wallace said, whistling the *Ghostbusters* theme song.

"Free drinks on the cruises?" Jeanine interrupted.

"I don't think they mention that in the package, but I can definitely get them to throw that in. But only if you decide within a week."

"What? Slither back to sea, ya bilge rat." Jeanine shot up and headed inside, stopping in the doorway when Mr. Wallace spoke again.

"Listen, if I may, folks…it's a sweet deal. I know you love this place. I know you love its history. I know these are original homes for some of you, but life does move on, and in most people's cases, it does so without benefit or fanfare. At least you'll be receiving some very nice compensation."

I thought of Aunt Sylvie and what she would want to do in this situation. If I left it to my mother, she'd sell the house in a heartbeat.

"You'd be taken care of for the rest of your lives," Mr. Wallace added. "Atlantis is dedicated to making sure you're happy. They're a good company, folks. You can email or call me if you have any other questions."

"When would they be ready to close?" Jax asked.

"Oh, you hush, boy," Heloise said, pressing back tears in her eyes. I gave her a sad smile. This couldn't be easy for her.

Mr. Wallace turned at the gate. "As soon as you are. Have a good day, everybody." He walked back to his car, leaving us all to stare at each other in silent, painful melancholy, like deer stunned with darts.

"What do we do?" Heloise asked.

"We stay, just like we said," Jeanine replied.

"But we always said we wanted to live on the ocean. With their package, we'd literally be on the ocean *all* the time," Heloise said. "Cruises for life? They're not making this easy on us, are they?"

"I love my house. I grew up in it. It meant everything to my parents," Jax said, "but he's right. Life goes on, and I don't know about you all, but I could use $1.5 million."

"Bah." Salty Sid waved us all away. "What good is money to most of us who are on our way out anyway?"

"Speak for yourself, geezer," Jeanine said.

"Oh, Sid, for goodness sake," Heloise added.

"Easy for you to say," Jax fired back. "I have a kid to pay for, to make proud of me. A kid who won't come visit no matter what I do for him, who thinks I'm a loser for not making enough. A business that could use a financial boost. You know what? Forget it." Jax stormed home, and part of me wanted to follow.

But this wasn't my fight. These beautiful people had to decide for themselves what was right, just as I did. As the rest of the neighbors dispersed, I quietly took one of Atlantis's manila envelopes off the porch railing and went home.

In the evening, I sat with a glass of Riesling out on the beach. A nearly full moon shone above the horizon, illuminating calm waters. The waves lapped quietly on the shore. After Mr. Wallace's visit, Heloise had burst into the house crying with Jeanine after her, while Salty Sid and I reviewed the cruise line's packet in my kitchen to make sure we'd heard everything right.

I resisted calling my mother to tell her about the rep's offer, because I knew she'd love it and would want to close the matter right away, whereas I wanted to simmer this a bit.

The good news was that this had to be a collaborative decision. Either they all decided to sell, or Atlantis couldn't buy. The bad news was...this had to be a collaborative decision. If only one resident didn't want to sell, it could create bad vibes among us all.

For whatever it was worth, I was on the fence. If this were my house, I'd be agonizing, too. It was a sweet deal, like Mr. Wallace said, but I also understood where Jeanine and Sid were coming from. There was an irreplaceable quality about this island, something that would be lost forever if Atlantis were to buy.

I sipped my wine and closed my eyes, trying to listen to my inner voice. Maybe the answer would come in meditation, like Jeanine and Heloise said.

After a few minutes, I sensed I wasn't alone and opened my eyes. Just the ocean, pooling her waves around my feet, and a few gulls nearby tearing apart a dead fish. I checked behind me, expecting to see Luna, but instead, nobody was there.

I sighed and finished the wine, and when I got up to go back inside, a woman was standing on the back porch. A white woman I'd never seen before with reddish-brown long hair, thick, dark eyebrows, and a strong chin. She was dressed in short pants, black boots up to her knees, and a white button-down shirt. In the crook of her elbow, she held a wicker basket filled with key limes.

For a moment, I felt disoriented. In my tipsy state, I couldn't remember if I'd walked down the beach and ended up at someone else's house. To throw me off even more, I thought I could hear that old-timey music again, as if playing out of a vintage record player. But no, this was still Aunt Sylvie's house, that was Bowie asleep next to her, and that was a stranger staring back at me.

"Can I help…" I couldn't finish the question.

The woman held her concerned expression and pointed toward the side of the house where Jeanine was coming around the bend, tapping a pack of cigarettes in her hand, and stopping at the tree with the glass ball ornament. The woman disappeared.

"Hey, Pulitzer."

"Did you…did you see that?"

"See what?"

"That woman. Right there on my porch. Holding a basket, pointing at you just as you were getting here. Did you see her?"

"Oh, you saw Annie." Jeanine plopped her butt on the sand and dropped her head in her hands. "Cool."

Cool? That's it?

A flash of memory, of me and Gary playing the Ouija board in the upstairs bedroom as kids, flashed through my mind. A-N-M? No, it'd spelled A-N-N, not A-N-M, and the spirit we'd contacted was Rumrunning Annie?

"Is that supposed to be normal? I mean, I...I'm pretty sure I just saw a ghost." I looked back at the porch again, hoping she'd reappear, but only Luna was there now, watching Bowie in his sleep.

"You did. It's her house."

"It's my house. Sylvie's house, I mean," I retorted. "Isn't that a little...I don't know...strange?"

"Yes, but strange is de facto here, Pulitzer. You know that. I'm surprised it took you this long to see her. You've been here, what, three weeks?"

"Almost a month."

"She usually makes herself known by opening or closing doors and moving things around the house," she said. I thought back to the windows opening and the sun hat appearing out of nowhere. "Anyway, figured I'd find you out here."

"Where's Heloise?" I sat next to her, but still checked the back porch in case I saw Annie again.

So that was the famous rumrunner of Skeleton Key. Part of me now wondered if she'd been looking at me at all. Maybe I'd just watched a reenactment of her pointing down the beach at rumrunners washing up on her shore. Maybe I'd just peered into the past.

"Inside, drowning her sorrows. I asked if she wanted to come out, but she's so broken up over this."

"Why, though? You guys don't want to sell. Neither does Sid. Jax is obviously on the fence."

"Because, the word around the island is that most residents are over the moon about the new deal," Jeanine said. "Even the ones who didn't want to sell before changed their minds right quick. Sellouts."

"That's what the cruise line intended, obviously," I said, "to drive a hard bargain."

"They must be doing witchcraft back there at corporate, or something," Jeanine said, drawing from her cigarette. "Little voodoo dolls of all the residents, pricking them with pins to make them change their minds."

I giggled. "Money talks. That's all it is."

"Some things are more important."

"I agree." I sighed. "But as long as even one homeowner doesn't want to sell, it's a no-go, right? I mean, what are they going to do, build around one house?" I buried my feet in the sand. "So just tell Mr. Wallace that Atlantis is screwed. The end."

"Not that easy, Pulitzer. See, that's where the peer pressure begins. We don't want to be the ones responsible for making twenty-two other homeowners unhappy. We've been fielding calls all day from other residents asking us to sell, even the ones who are never here."

"I'm sorry. That must suck."

"It does. What's Sylvie going to do?"

I hadn't told Jeanine yet about Sylvie's inability to make decisions. It was all on her power of attorney, and knowing my conservative mother, without any emotional ties to this house, we knew how that would go.

"Actually, Jeanine." I thought about the best way to break the news. "My aunt has Alzheimer's, apparently. I hadn't told you yet. I'm sorry. I know you were good friends with her."

Jeanine's eyes regarded me a moment then she turned and took another drag from her cigarette. "We knew Sylvie wasn't coming back."

"How did you know?"

"She left everything here. She would've wanted her stuff, her Tarot cards, books, all her things." She threw her hands up. "Ah, screw it. All the more reason to sell. No use fighting the end of an era."

"What? That doesn't sound like you. Where's the spunky Jeanine I know and love, huh?"

"Pulitzer, Heloise wants to sell."

"What?" Well, that changed everything. "She does?"

"Says we have to move with the changing times. We can't get stuck in the past, and resisting change is pointless. Gah, I don't know what to think."

"But you guys love this place with all your heart. You adore this island. It's…it's your little bubble." I felt a quiver of panic deep in my chest. If Jeanine was giving up, it would start a chain reaction, and soon, this island would become Cabana Cay.

I almost barfed just thinking about it.

"It is. I'm torn up about it. Our life here won't ever have a price tag. Like, if we lived in a condo, where would we have our bonfires?"

"Exactly."

"We won't be allowed to have moon parties on the beach, that's for sure. Where are we supposed to put our garden gnomes? Our herb garden? We'd have a place to live, but we'd still be homeless." Her hands shook so much, I reached out to take one.

"I couldn't empathize with you more," I said, thinking of my home—my *house*—in Long Island. Even if I won it in court, it'd never be the same.

"Where will we meditate? Where will we dance naked?" she laughed, brushing her lower lid with her thumb. "The life we've built for ourselves these last twenty years will be gone, Pulitzer. There's no enchantment in a new building. But now Heloise is saying it's wrong of us to resist change. She said, 'Look at Lily and how she's stuck in the past. What kind of people would we be if we tell her to move on, but then we can't move on?'"

"Oh, gosh." My face dropped. "Because this life *is* worth fighting for, Jeanine. The one I need to let go of *isn't*. Huge difference. Tell her that."

"It's out of my hands, cupcake." Jeanine stood and brushed sand off her butt. "The house may be in both our names, but this is Heloise's family home. I can't make that decision for her. I'm going to go see how she's doing."

"Jeanine, wait."

She turned.

What was I about to say? That I agreed with her? That it would pain me to see this island turned into a commercialized resort? That I, too, had been having dreams of more...

"Did you know that Sylvie had a dream of turning her home into a bed-and-breakfast?"

A sad smile crossed her face. She gazed at the ocean. "Yeah. We all did. We used to talk about it all the time, how we'd work there together, host dinners, make pies, happiness, and magic for the rest of our lives."

I watched the wistful expression on her face fade away.

"It was just a pipe dream. Reality always wins out in the end, don't it? See you later, Pulitzer."

18

I'd been dreaming about Annie.

Standing on the back porch, pointing down the beach. She never spoke aloud, but she was trying to tell me something. Every time I got close to her, though, it would start raining. Storming. And every time the deluge fell, the sand would clear, exposing more of the covered boardwalk. When I uncovered the entire boardwalk, it stretched for miles in either direction. Before I could see where it led, the rainwater would rise up my legs, past my mouth, nearly drowning me.

Finally, I awoke in a heavy sweat.

Damn hot flashes.

The window had blown wide open, and the curtains billowed horizontally into the room. In the moonlight, Bowie's curious green eye and blue eye watched them surge. The air smelled of sweet and salty humidity. A rainstorm was moving in, electrical charge in the air.

"Thanks, I was burning up," I said to whoever—Annie?

Now I was talking to a ghost in the dark, in the middle of the night. When my mother suggested I'd come to Skeleton Key to find sanity, little did she know just how much I'd shed my old self.

The new me was finding that she loved new things. Like a rainstorm on the horizon. Or that sometimes, the best way to prepare meals was using no-frills methods. That some men actually found me to be intimidating. That I loved silence more than I'd realized. That sex magic sounded interesting. That ghost cats were comforting. That spirits of rumrunning women inspired me.

I sat up and rubbed my eyes.

Apparently, full nights of sleep were now a thing of the past. Thank you, fluctuating estrogen levels. On the bed next to me were Sylvie's photo albums and journals. I'd been perusing them before falling asleep. I'd gotten to the pages marked "binding spells" and "hexes" when I had to close the journal. It had felt too personal. I'd never believed in witchcraft before, yet here I was, enthralled with Sylvie's private world.

I checked the time.

4 AM. I wouldn't be falling asleep again any time soon. Not after that dream.

I opened the journal. *Manifestation*, Sylvie had written in big, loopy letters I'd only ever seen inside greeting cards on my birthdays and holidays. Following that heading were several other "spells" for bringing things into fruition. I half-expected to see eye of newt or wart of toad on there, but they were simple, everyday things I could find in the house.

"Beach Spell," I read aloud, "to be performed near the full moon." I looked out the window. The moon was bright but would soon be covered by clouds. Other ingredients: *a stick, sand, sugar.* The steps were simple. All I had to do was go outside under the waxing moon, preferably on a Sunday night (or Thursday, if I'd be asking for money), and use my intention.

"Bo, want to try some magic?" I climbed off the bed and carried the journal downstairs, hoping I wouldn't run into Annie along the way. As peaceful as she'd felt to me, I still didn't want to run into a kickass woman in the dark. I should've been shocked to see Luna curled up in the back window, which had also decided to open on its own.

But I wasn't. At all.

Bowie wasn't surprised either. He watched her without growling, and seeing that she wasn't going to threaten him, he decided to get a snack.

"Do you have anything to say to me today?" I asked and waited.

When Luna didn't respond, I grabbed sugar, went into the garden to find a stick, found the mermaid fountain staring at me somewhat impatiently, and quickly closed the door.

"Sheesh." I got the distinct feeling that she wanted to be restored, like now, like everything else around this house. "Fine, I'll buy outdoor enamel tomorrow." I felt like I was losing my mind.

All I needed was sand and moonlight, but the storm clouds kept rolling in, partially covering up the moon. Not sure if the spell would work, cringing at my own thought that it even might. What was I doing? Following Sylvie's directions written in her journals, I closed my eyes and tried to imagine a purple-gold light floating over me, cleansing me of unwanted energy or stress.

I had to face east and thank the element of Air for joining me. I was supposed to ask Air to help me with my manifestation, but I felt bizarre doing that, so I just turned ninety degrees south and did the same with the element of Fire. Thanking Fire, asking it to help me. Then, I turned west, facing the back of the house, and asked the element of Water to join me, to bestow some of her fluidity, love, and purity of emotion. Then I did the same for north and Earth.

Bowie followed me out. He stood on the perimeter of the beach, watching me like I was insane. Maybe I was. With the wind whipping my hair, and the heat swirling around me, rustling of trees, ocean waves, and wind all churning together, I felt like the elements had heard my plea. I was supposed to draw a pentagram in the sand with the stick, but that didn't feel right.

What if I summoned something evil?

You won't.

Looking back, I saw Luna in the window, cracking open an eye at me.

"What am I doing, Bo? Bo, what am I doing?" I asked desperately, feeling madness well up inside me. Bowie had no answers, but he was dying to see what I'd do next, pupils dilated, drawing in the darkness.

"Spirit, please help me draw a circle around me, for bringing sweetness into my life."

I read Sylvie's incantation aloud, word for word, and used the sugar to make a huge circle in the sand. After that, I sat in the middle facing the ocean and thought about everything I wanted to draw into my life. Apparently, the full moon was about fullest potential. Time to ask the universe for big things.

I'd make a list in the morning, but for now, all that came to mind was: *Make a name for myself that doesn't involve Weasel.*

Bowie crossed the circle line and crawled into my lap. Did I have to redo the circle now that he'd crossed it? So much I didn't know.

Stand on my own two feet without Weasel.
Make my children proud.
Pay for my children's college without help.
And finally…
Find a new home and restaurant space.

With the stick, I was supposed to write keywords in the sand or draw something if I liked, so I drew a house with a chimney and tree beside it, just like I used to do when I was little. I drew flowers and a Bowie that looked more like Godzilla.

Bowie sat on my drawing.

"It's not fat. It's fluff," I nudged him away and redrew his picture. I was about to add a restaurant to my sand sketch when the wind picked up, blowing grit everywhere and ruining everything.

Maybe Air wasn't having it.

Maybe I shouldn't be dabbling with things I didn't understand.

I was about to get up and leave when I read Sylvie's note at the bottom: *Thank the elements and close the circle.*

I wasn't sure how to do that, so I did what felt most normal—faced each direction, thanking earth, water, fire, and air in reverse, feeling stupid and in need of a manifestation tutor. Whatever, I would ask Heloise and Jeanine how to do this right. I shouldn't have tried on my own.

I erased what was left of the sugar circle, picked up the bag, and headed back to the house, but something made me pause. I looked up at the house, expecting to see Annie again. But a light was on in my upstairs window. It pulsated once, twice, then went dark. At almost the same time, another rogue wind whipped across the beach, wrapped around me, then disappeared.

I stood there a few minutes, too nervous to go inside.

What if Annie didn't want me here? What if I didn't vibe with her home or wasn't the right kind of witch, or wasn't a very good one at all? I was a city slicker. I had considered, for a moment, telling Sylvie to sell her home. When I saw Annie pointing, could that have meant she wanted me to go?

"I don't think we should sell, Annie," I said, "just in case you were wondering. I actually think this whole island has huge potential. For what yet, I'm not sure."

I couldn't let the spirit of a long-gone woman scare me. I lived here now. I was the one taking care of the house. Annie should be happy someone cared about it. Deep down, I knew the rumrunner wasn't upset. I couldn't explain the feeling I had walking back into the house and up the stairs, holding Bowie in my arms for comfort, but it wasn't fear. It was sadness, like the way you feel when an old Hollywood actor passes, when you know a golden era has come to an end.

Like things will never be the same again.

But you're glad for having experienced them.

In the morning, I'd decided now might be a good time to try that sex magic. It started out perfectly fine—I gave myself permission to think about my kiss with Jax, the way his body shone with a layer of sweat when he was washing down his boat, how much I wished I were his boat sometimes.

Everything was going fine, except something wasn't right. I couldn't put my finger on it. All I knew was that

Bowie wasn't curled up asleep at the foot of the bed like he'd been lately after I knocked him into the headboard space that time. He was staring at me intensely, ruining any chance I had of working up sexual energy.

To further cockblock, my phone rang.

My mother, calling me shortly after sunrise?

"Hello," I answered groggily.

"Sorry to wake you, Lily," Mom said.

I wasn't ready to chit-chat this early in the day, but I supposed the timing was fine. Atlantis's offer package sat on my nightstand, and I couldn't keep the news of the cruise rep's visit to myself much longer.

"No worries. I didn't sleep well last night, and there was this weird electrical storm that didn't manifest into anything. Meaning, it never rained, but then this weird wind—"

"Lily, dear, your Aunt Sylvie passed away."

My breath caught in my throat. My pulse began throbbing in my ears. "What?"

"Early this morning, 3 AM. Her nurse called an hour ago." Her voice cracked. She sniffled, and then my mother was full-on sobbing.

My mouth hung open, as I stared at the brightness outside the window, which had behaved and stayed shut when I closed it last night. We knew this was coming, but it still felt like a surprise. "I'm so sorry, Mom."

"You're never quite prepared for these things, even when you think you are. I thought I'd never cry again after losing Gary. Lord knows nothing could be worse than that, but losing Sylvie is just…well…my entire childhood, Lil."

"Oh, Mom." I finally said. "I know how that feels."

"I know you do, honey."

"I was awake at that time, by the way." It was after the dream that had woken me up in a wave of hot flashes. I'd been reading Aunt Sylvie's spell book. Wait…

You don't suppose you caused it, did you, Lily?

The horror came to me like a pin dropped in silence.

No…

A voice filtered through my mind. Loving, sweet, wise.

Aunt Sylvie?

You've done nothing wrong, Lily. Thank you.

Not Annie's voice, but my aunt's. I never recognized it until now. I never imagined it could be her. She'd been alive until early this morning, after all.

Being dead is not a requirement for haunting someone, I recalled Jeanine telling me a while back. Could it have been Sylvie all this time, speaking to me? After all, she'd been in a dream state of sorts. Was it possible she'd been communicating with me in her condition?

Mom was rattling on about paperwork she needed to fill out, arrangements to be made, whereas I couldn't stop recalling the bizarre, sleepless night I'd had, how I'd found the courage to do things I'd never done before. Never even *thought* of doing before. A beach spell for manifestation? Me? Really?

"After you mentioned how you wanted to go see her, I got to thinking maybe I should fly down one more time to visit. I even told your father about the possibility of me going alone, and now this happens." Mom sobbed again.

"Mom, it's okay. Like you told me, it's better to remember her in her happier days. I've been doing that a lot, since I found her photo albums. It's just a coincidence that I happened to be awake at that time."

I thought back to how the light upstairs had flickered. How I'd felt something go through me. Had that been Sylvie? Had the soul of my beautiful, hippie aunt passed away then flown down to Skeleton Key to see her home one more time? If I had a one-way ticket to the Great Wherever, I'd do the same.

I came to say goodbye.

Oh, Sylvie. I blinked, releasing tears I hadn't realized had formed. Why didn't we act on our instincts enough? Why had it taken me so long to go visit her? I broke down, while Mom mostly talked to herself.

Finally, she sniffed, her voice regaining composure. "I suppose I can finally tell you this." There was renewed, no-nonsense business in her voice. "Aunt Sylvie left the house to you, dear."

My lungs stopped working. Bowie walked over to me and peered deep into my eyes. I scratched him between the ears. I finally let air into my lungs, but I couldn't process what Mom had said.

"I'm sorry, what?" I dropped the phone, picked it back up upside-down, then turned it around again. "Hello? You still there?"

"Yes, did you hear what I said, Lily? Your Aunt Sylvie...she left me cash, stocks, and personal things from our childhood, but to you, she left the house."

"The house," I stammered. "The house I'm currently in?"

"For heaven's sake, I can see it was too early to call you. You're in a fog of confusion."

"Mom, I'm just...a little shook, okay? I can't believe it." This house was mine? I could sell it or live in it or do whatever I wanted with it? I had a home, after all?

I had a home after all.

"Are you sure?"

"Of course, I'm sure. You're Lily Autumn Blanchett, aren't you? That's what it says right here. 'And to my only niece, I bequeath my homestead property on 111 Key Lime Lane, Skeleton Key, Florida.'"

"The house is mine," I repeated. I stared around the room, at the little beach cottage by the sea. At part of my childhood. I saw Sylvie dancing on the sand, Gary's sandcastles, little me thrashing in the surf. "It's mine."

"I'm happy with her decision, Lily. It makes perfect sense. She always thought of you as her child—a child who only visited once a year—but her child nonetheless. And you *were* the closest thing to a daughter that she had." Again, her voice broke off at the end. "I know that's an extra responsibility you weren't expecting. Sell it immediately if you don't want to be troubled with it."

"It's fine, Mom. Really, it is. No trouble at all."

Not one tiny little bit.

In fact, from the moment I'd arrived, the little house on Skeleton Key had been nothing but a pleasure. A pleasure to live in, a pleasure to fix up, a pleasure to revive—from the interior, to the garden, to its "idiosyncrasies" and the energy within. I couldn't help but feel like I'd been sent down to bring the house on Key Lime Lane back to life.

But who would've guessed that instead, the house would revive *me*?

19

The next day, Jeanine caught me as I was getting into my car. "Hey, Pulitzer, you know Nanette on Coconut Court?"

"Haven't met her yet."

"Well, meeting at her house, 2 PM, to discuss the cruise line's offer and get a headcount of who's yeah, and who's nay."

"Do I have to go?" I asked like a scared nine-year-old.

"Oh, that's right. You don't own the house. I guess not," she said. "See you later."

I could've told her right then that Sylvie's house was now mine, but I was scared to. For some reason, I felt stuck in limbo, afraid of moving forward, knowing that when I did, everything would change.

Was I ready for everyone to know?

I went to Michaels with the intention of delaying the inevitable and to purchase outdoor paints for the mermaid statue, and, upon returning to Skeleton Key, considered heading straight to the side yard to get to work but felt guilty. I couldn't skip a town hall meeting. Not about something so important. I was a forty-five-year old adult who needed to face responsibilities, not hide at home.

I didn't know which was Nanette's house on Coconut Court, but I guessed by how many people were sitting in folding chairs on her lawn, deep in loud discussion. Nanette, I took it, was the older lady standing on a wooden crate, getting everyone to shush down. I parked and walked up to the house.

Heloise saw me and waved me over to a shady spot under an umbrella tree.

"Hi," I whispered. "Can I talk to you guys a minute?"

"We're starting, Lily. Can it wait?" Heloise flipped my hair. "Girl, you're looking cute today. The Keys have been good to you."

"No doubt about that," I replied.

Salty Sid was there, talking to neighbors. He waved at me from across the yard. I couldn't see Jax anywhere. "Where's the captain?" I whispered.

"Not now, Pulitzer. This isn't *Love Connection*." Jeanine rolled her eyes.

I scoffed. "I was asking because he's a resident, Jeanini Panini. Geez." I knew how to take a hint. I would shut up now and tell them about Aunt Sylvie later.

"Alright, ladies and gentlemen. By now, I trust you've all had a chance to go over Atlantis Cruise Line's very generous package," Nanette said loudly. "And I know this hasn't been easy, but if I know the people of Skeleton Key, I know you care about your home very much. By show of hands, how many of you are considering accepting the package, a.k.a. selling your home to Atlantis?"

I sensed a collective holding of breath across the lawn, as most hands went up. I couldn't say I was surprised. The offer was rather generous, but I was surprised to see Heloise and

Jeanine's hands up as well. Salty Sid's hand stayed firmly tucked into his crossed arms.

The crowd of twenty or so homeowners fell into a chatter, as Nanette tried to regain their attention.

I looked at Jeanine and Heloise. "You're kidding me, right?"

Jeanine shrugged. "It's out of my hands, girl. And besides, Nanette did say 'considering.'"

I turned to my other side. "Heloise? Why?" I asked, surprised by the hurt in my voice. Why did this feel personal, as though I'd lived here all my life? "You love this neighborhood. This is your family's home."

"Free cruises for life is hard to ignore," Heloise said, "especially for someone who loves the ocean as much as I do."

"Free drinks," Jeanine added.

"Heloise, those cruises are packed with people, annoying loud music, and way too many screaming kids running around without their parents. You sure you want that?" I didn't know whether or not that was true, but I had a picture to paint. "You already have the ocean right here."

"Shh." Jeanine leaned into my ear.

"You, shh," I retorted.

Nanette went on. "Looks like most of us are onboard, with the exception of the young lady in the blue shirt." I glanced around looking for the young woman in blue, only to find that everyone was looking at me. "What's your name?"

"Me? Uh, Lily, here representing my aunt, Sylvie Collier of 111 Key Lime Lane."

"Ah, you're the famous gourmand, Lily Blanchett." She said it in a way that set off a titter of chuckles across the lawn.

187

I felt my stomach clench. How many of these people had seen the drama of my marriage unfold all over the Internet and believed I was unstable?

"So, then Sylvie Collier, represented by Lily Blanchett, plus Sid Roberts are not in favor of selling their homes," Nanette said. Everyone broke into good-natured laughter.

"Why is that funny?" I whispered to Jeanine.

She leaned into me. "Sid doesn't own a house on the island. He owns a houseboat, but we consider him one of our residents. It's all on your aunt, Lily." She placed her arm around my shoulder. "No pressure."

She had to be kidding me. What happened to residents loving their island? What happened to not selling out? I couldn't believe this decision was falling on me.

"Excuse me, I just need a minute." And then, I charged out of there, going for a walk around the block.

Jeanine and Heloise met me on the corner, so by the time I'd made one round of mindless speedwalking, I ran into them again.

"Lily," Jeanine wheezed. "Don't lose sleep over this, babe. We know your mother handles Sylvie's affairs. We'd hoped you'd be able to change her mind, but after that offer, looks like it was us who changed our minds."

I held onto a stop sign for support. "Jeanine, Heloise, there's something I need to tell you." I looked at both their concerned faces, hands shielding their eyes from the sun.

"I know," Heloise said. "I felt it last night. What did I tell you, babe?"

"What?" I asked. "That my aunt passed away? Because she did. Early this morning at 3 AM."

"I knew it." Heloise pressed her fingertips to her eyes. "I knew this would happen."

"I can't believe it. Sylvie's gone?" Jeanine walked in a tight circle. "We should've gone to visit her. We took too long."

"I know. I feel the same way. But there's something else...the house? It's now mine. Aunt Sylvie left her house to me. I'm the one who needs to make a decision about the sale, not her, not my mother."

That was one that Heloise hadn't counted on. Both watched me like that was the last thing they'd ever expected.

Jeanine let out a slow whistle. "Well, then, it's a done deal. Because we knew from the beginning you wanted Sylvie to sell," Jeanine said, heartbreak in her eyes. "You've been fixing the place up since you got here."

"Not necessarily to sell, Jeanine. My mother had been considering keeping the house for rental as well. Don't make me a villain here. You saw me not raise my hand over there. Me, I've fallen in love with the house."

There, I said it.

Their faces examined mine. "What does this mean, Lily?"

I could hear the wheels turning in their heads. If I sold, Atlantis would have itself a home for Cabana Cay, but if I kept the house, all these fine people, who now included Heloise and Jeanine, would be screwed out of an amazing package. If I decided to stay, I would have to convince them that their homes were worth saving.

I moved under the shade of a banyan tree, and the ladies followed. Heloise broke out her paper fan. "Heavens, what are we going to do now? I didn't see this one coming."

"Hear me out," I said. "I've been thinking about this all day. What if I don't sell? What if I stay?"

"Why would you want to stay, Pulitzer? I'm not upset, obviously, but I need to know," Jeanine said.

"Because. I've been here nearly six weeks, and I've grown to love this place. Not just the house, but the island, the people, the beach, the starry nights, the lapping of waves, the flowers, the vibe, the laughter, the moon parties, the unnamable quality of Skeleton Key, you guys. Everything."

Heloise fanned herself, then me, then Jeanine. "But you have a life back in New York. You have plans to open a new restaurant, don't you?"

"I don't have anything right now. That's what makes this the perfect decision. You guys were right about the house. I don't want it. Weasel can keep that. As for a new restaurant, I can open one anywhere, doesn't have to be in NYC."

"But wouldn't you want to sell your aunt's house and buy yourself a nice little spot for you and the kids back home?" Heloise asked.

"Didn't you hear the girl? She's in love with Skeleton Key," Jeanine laughed. "This outdated, trapped-in-time little island. She's in love with it." Jeanine stood behind Heloise where her wife couldn't see her and pumped a fist in the air.

"It's not about the money, Heloise. I've grown to genuinely love this place. And sifting through Sylvie's things reminded me of a dream I used to have when I was little."

"The bed-and-breakfast," she guessed.

"Yes."

"But that was Sylvie's dream," Heloise said. "And Sylvie's no longer here, bless her heart, but I feel like you might be doing this out of respect for your aunt, not because you really want to stay."

"I really want to stay," I said.

Yes, Jeanine mouthed.

"The bed-and-breakfast was my dream, too, when I was little. I used to draw it in the sand. But as time went by, I forgot about it. That happens, doesn't it? As we get older, we forget our childhood dreams, but that's the one time in our lives when things are most magical."

"That's very true." Heloise nodded.

"Growing up dampens our fullest potential," I said.

"And you're sure a bed-and-breakfast on Skeleton Key will do well?" she asked.

"Absolutely. There's this trend. I'm sure you've seen it if you watch enough cooking and travel TV. Spooky-themed, monster-themed, haunted-themed restaurants, circuses, even bars, some of them based on popular dark or fantasy books or film. For a while, I thought if I opened one myself, it would be a spooky-style restaurant. But what if it isn't?"

"What if it's Sylvie's house," Jeanine caught on to my idea, her eyes lighting up. Yes, at least one person onboard, and from her secretive smile, I could tell this might be the thing to change Heloise's mind. "Go on, Pulitzer."

"I'm having trouble wrapping my head around this," Heloise said.

"Have you ever seen Christine McConnell?" I asked. "She bakes creepy cookies, had her own TV show for a while. She does crafts, builds large-scale displays for Halloween, and such?"

"Okay…"

"The gothic, witchy aesthetic has become quite trendy, but for us…" I raised an eyebrow. "It's not just a trend. It's real."

Jeanine pointed to me. "That's what I'm talking about!"

"Heloise, can't you see it? You and Jeanine can make key lime pies, coconut cream pies, shrimp scampi, all your amazing breakfasts, muffins, brunches, and such. Sid can give historical tours of the island, Jax can take them for chartered boat rides. We can make moon parties an actual thing for guests looking for a witchy experience. Moonlight meditation on the beach. Yoga, the whole nine yards."

"Oo, yoga!" Jeanine squealed.

"We can do this," I said. "With my connections, a few well-placed promo spots in magazines and travel shows, my daughter Emily doing the marketing, my son Chase doing…I don't know what, but I'll think of something."

"A family-owned business?" Heloise looked at me then Jeanine.

"Yes!" I loved that. Family-owned. I hadn't felt excited for anything like this in a long time. "I would pay you, of course. We could split proceeds. I don't care. Name your terms."

"Oh, she's going all boss lady on us." Heloise nudged Jeanine, but the laughter was back in her voice.

"Think about it. Even if we all sell our homes, Atlantis won't let us do moon parties anymore. It'd be their beach. They won't let us make bonfires. They won't let Sid come around selling his Catch of the Day anymore."

"Especially not with his *Get Leid* hat," Jeanine snarked.

"They won't let Jax run a business from their property," Heloise said.

"He barely runs one now," Jeanine murmured.

"We can change that," I said. "With the publicity I know I can get us, we can help him get his biz up and running. I've been talking to him. He's going to modernize his practices and strategies. Guys, this could be incredibly rewarding! We get to have our cake and eat it, too."

"I like cake," Heloise said.

"What kind of cake is it?" Jeanine asked.

"Any kind!" I said.

"Can we make it the witch-themed bed and breakfast? I really liked that one." Jeanine rubbed her hands together like an old crone over a cozy, warm fire.

"Let's talk about it. I don't know why I never mentioned my idea to you before. I guess I never expected to see both your hands up in that meeting. That really surprised me." I frowned.

"Yeah, why didn't you?" Heloise gave me side-eye.

"For one, I didn't own the house," I said.

But Heloise still needed convincing. "True. But Lily, something is niggling in the back of my head. I can't help but think you're only saying this to make a buck, but then soon, you'll find someone to run the B&B for you, then you'll take off again, and mark my words, when that happens, all that magic you're talking about will—poof—be out the door. What makes that home magical now…"

"Is you," Jeanine finished.

"I won't be out the door," I said. "I'm a lot of things, Heloise—a workaholic, a denier of truth sometimes, unconfident, dumb when it comes to men—but one thing I am not is disloyal. If that were true, I would've sold *Chelsea Garden Grill* a long time ago to make a buck."

"Haven't you heard her agonizing over losing the restaurant for six weeks now, babe?" Jeanine said. "That place was her baby. This here girl puts her heart and soul into everything she does. Plus, she's letting go of the past, like we taught her. She's starting fresh and new."

"Guys, I'm really excited about this." I beamed. "I'm in love with Skeleton Key. More than that, I'm in love with this idea. I'm in love with me, for once. I *will* run the place myself. I *will* stay indefinitely."

It was the first time I'd said that loud. Even Jeanine smiled bigger than I'd ever seen her. Her wild eyes loaded up with tears and she nodded. "Pulitzer, you continue to surprise me."

I took Heloise's hands. "I'll still live right over there, right up in Sylvie's room, with the light that turns on and off at will." I pointed in the direction of home.

Home.

I loved the idea of a witch-themed bed-and-breakfast. We had the ghost of an independent woman way before her time, we had a ghost cat, we had a mermaid statue who stared at anyone within range, we had witchy neighbors, we had a boat named the *Sea Witch*, we had a woke fisherman any feminist would love…we had it all.

Even Bogey and Bacall.

"Heloise…" I looked into her eyes. "It'll be like you, Jeanine, Sylvie, and Aurelia, Jax's mom, all over again. Our own little coven, except no one has to know that. The dream will be real, except it'll be me instead of Sylvie. That's okay, isn't it? I know I'm not her. It's not perfect, but…"

"But it's pretty damn good. And to be honest, you're better at manifesting than your aunt was. No offense to you, Sylvie." Jeanine blew a kiss into the sky. "But your witchy niece has got it going on!" She clapped enthusiastically, until Heloise shot her a look.

Witchy. Me? If by witchy, Jeanine meant someone who took charge of her life and the necessary steps to bring her dreams to fruition, helping those around her on the way up, then I'd wear that label proudly.

What do you think of that, Sylvie?

After reading mine and Jeanine's faces for a minute and looking back at the meeting still in session, Heloise sighed. "You two do make a compelling pitch, I have to say."

"So, you'll consider it?" I asked. "Let's have a moon party tonight and discuss it more. I'll make lobster with French lemon butter sauce. I've still got jumbo shrimp I bought from Sid, and I won't make a key lime pie. I promise."

I had to pull out all the stops to convince Heloise. It was true that as long as I didn't want to sell, the cruise line couldn't touch us. But I wanted Heloise to be happy. I didn't want her to hate me for the rest of her life. I wanted this to be a fresh start for all of us.

"Let's see what Grandmamá says about it," she sighed.

"Grandmamá?" I raised an eyebrow.

"Oh, Lily. I love that you still don't know it all."

I smiled. "I like the sound of that."

20

"When I need a question answered, I'll ask her three or four times within a few days." Heloise led us onto the beach area next to my house adjacent to hers. We came to a stop at the coconut palm with the glass ball hanging from it. "Here we are."

"This is Grandmamá?" I looked at the blue-green blown glass ball wrapped in muslin rope wound tightly around the tree that I'd seen at least a dozen times in the past six weeks. "I didn't know this belonged to you. I always assumed it was a decoration my aunt left."

"Nope," Heloise said. "My grandmother gave me this ornament over forty years ago when she visited from the Bahamas. It's been hanging here about thirty of those years. Whenever I need guidance, I come out here, meditate on my grandmother's wisdom, and swing the ball lightly. If it goes right to left, it's one answer. If it goes back to front, it's another."

"It's a pendulum," Jeanine explained.

I'd read about pendulums in Sylvie's journal. In fact, I'd found several in her vanity chest in the spare bedroom close. It reminded me of the old wives' trick of using a paper clip hanging from a string to tell if a baby would be a boy or a girl. "How do you know which answer she gives?"

"You'll see." She unwound the ball from the tree, held it in her hands, and closed her eyes. Jeanine and I watched on from a respectful distance. After a long minute of silent tuning in, Heloise called, "Chère, Grandmamá, I know I've asked you this a few times in the last few days, but I need to know...should I stay or should I go?"

Jeanine broke into giggles.

I shot her a look through my own smile.

"If you think I should sell the house, swing left and right. If you think I should stay, swing back and forth." She set the ball swinging in a circular path and waited until it settled into a back-and-forth groove. "She says stay."

"Last time she said go," Jeanine told me. "She must've changed her mind when she heard your idea."

"What about the bed-and-breakfast?" I whispered.

"Chère Grandmamá," Heloise said again. "Miss Sylvie's niece, Lily, would like to convert her home into a bed-and-breakfast. Says it would be fun for all of us to run together, and I have to say, it does sound like an interesting premise. Should we do it? Left to right for yes, back and forth for no."

Again, she set the ball spinning in a wide circle, and I was sure it would settle on back-and-forth again, considering gravity and the same way Heloise had spun it the first time, but sure as sugar, it settled into a different path—left to right.

"She says yes."

"Thank you, Grandmamá," I said.

"We thank you for your guidance, Grandmamá." She wrapped the glass ball back around the tree and tucked it under a coil of rope to keep it anchored. "Well, the oracle has spoken."

My phone rang in my pocket. Carmen calling. "Guys, I'll see you in a bit. I have to take this." Leaving Heloise and Jeanine to discuss the future on the beach, I made my way toward the house, remembering I'd left the car at Nanette's. "Carmencita," I answered. "What's up?"

"Lily, do you have a minute?" There was trepidation in her voice. Whenever Carmen called, I imagined the restaurant burning down in crispy flames.

"Is everything okay?"

"Your ex is crazy. I'm so through with him, I can't even."

"What happened?" I entered the house through the side door, finding Bowie belly up in the middle of the floor. Five feet away was Luna, belly up in the middle of the floor.

"You remember how he hired that assistant without asking me?"

"Yes?"

"Well, the bitch took off after a week, making off with half the money in the assets account."

"WHAT?" I spun and faced the kitchen. Carmen's voice felt farther away than ever before. Another place and lifetime I used to know.

"I don't know, Lil, but she did. I went into the inventory account today to make a purchase for a new standup mixer, 'cause our old one finally gave out, and right there was a withdrawal posted two days ago for twenty grand, and the lady is gone. I'm done. Done with him."

"Does Derek know?" My hands were shaking.

"Yes. The cops have already come. We filed a report. It's all in his hands, Lily. I can't with him. I warned him I didn't like her. I told him he shouldn't hire anyone without the proper protocol that you and I came up with to prevent stuff like this. Without a background check. He seemed to feel they weren't necessary. He basically told me to shut up, that he knew what he was doing."

"And now we're twenty grand in the hole." I stared at the fridge, as I listened to Carmen go into detail about all the troubles she'd had with Derek in the last week alone. With both feet out of *Chelsea Garden Grill*'s door, I felt powerless to help.

Did it matter anymore?

Carmen sighed. "I don't know where I'm going from here. Without a paycheck, I don't know how long I'll get to keep living in Brooklyn. Dade and I aren't living together, and I don't know that we ever will be. I'm sure he'll let me stay at his place for a while, but eventually, I'm going to need to enact a Plan B."

Sounded to me like Dade needed to pop the question if he wanted to keep Carmen in his life, but I wasn't going to say that. "Come here with me."

"Where?"

"In the Florida Keys."

"What am I going to do there, Lil? No offense, but I graduated from Cornell School of Hospitality with the intention of making it big in the City."

"Yeah, and I got married to Derek Blanchett intending to stay married for a lifetime thinking I'd be at *Garden Grill* the rest of my life. Plans change, Carmen. Come stay with me a while. I'm putting together an idea that I think you will like."

"What's that?"

"You know."

"The haunted restaurant?"

"I'm going to turn my aunt's house into a bed-and-breakfast. A witch-themed bed-and-breakfast, and I'm going to need a staff to help me."

"You want me to come to the end of the world to help you run a tiny little B&B?"

"A witchy-themed one, yes. I have it all planned out."

"I have to say, Lil, you sound both completely off your rocker and refreshingly genius at the same time."

"That's how brilliance is born, isn't it? So will you come?" I crossed my fingers.

"I'll have to think about it. Right now, I'm packing. Not being at Chelsea, I already know I'm not going to be able to make my rent this month, so I'll call you soon from…I don't know. A park bench, an alleyway…"

"No, you'll find something. Stay with Dade for now. I know you. Nothing will keep you down for long," I said, then hung up. Carmen was a lot like me in that regard. She'd rise from the ashes in no time.

Well, Derek, you're in a heap of trouble, but it didn't surprise me. This was why I handled the business side of things for so long, because the day-to-day operations of a restaurant wasn't his forté. I felt sorry for him, but at the same time—screw that asshat. He deserved this for not listening to anyone but himself.

"But you know what?" I said to Bowie, coming around the corner. Luna was gone. Just Bowie looking at me, upside-down in Pet Me Mode. "It's not my problem anymore."

Outside, I heard the rumble of a truck pulling into the gravel driveway. Peeking through the blinds, I saw it was an unmarked van with a man stepping out of the driver's seat, a medium box in his hands. He hopped up the porch and was about to knock when the front door popped open all on its own.

The delivery man looked at me funny.

"Automatic doors." I smiled, holding out my hands.

"Lily Blanchett?" he asked, holding out his electronic notepad. "Could you sign here, please?"

Odd that someone would be sending me something to this address. Then I remembered the caftan I'd ordered and how it hadn't arrived yet. I scrawled my signature which never looked right on those narrow little screens and took the box.

"Hey, is this the old rumrunner distillery?" the young man asked.

"Annie Jackson's distillery? That's what they tell me," I replied. "Though it's been a normal house for the last forty years." *A haunted one, but normal.*

"My grandfather used to live near here years ago. Whenever I'd come to visit, he used to tell me this house was haunted, that the woman who lived here before you—not you—was a witch." He laughed. "The crazy things people tell kids, am I right?"

At that moment, another rogue breeze whipped around the porch, lifting the man's baseball cap right off his head. He caught it before it blew away.

"So crazy, right?" I gave him an evil smile. "Now scram."

"Yes, ma'am." He ran off without another comment, while I went back inside and set the box on top of the dining table. Already, I could see this table filled with guests, and Jeanine, Heloise, or I serving up dream menus for delighted out-of-towners. Salty Sid would give them the morning report and send them off to the Lower Keys in search of adventure.

I grabbed a knife from the kitchen and came back to open the box. Why would they put the caftan in a box? After all the peanuts and bubble wrap ended up on the floor, I was looking at a wooden box with a gold plate on it.

Not a caftan.

The name—Sylvie Beth Collier - 1944 - 2021.

"You're kidding me." As my hands shook, I lifted an envelope. Running my finger underneath the flap, I pulled out the black-and-white card and read aloud a note written in Sylvie's same loopy handwriting:

If you're reading this, it's because I'm on an everywhere-bound train to the Great Beyond. Do not mourn me. Celebrate. Please release me at my home on Skeleton Key.

- Sylvie Collier

Setting down the card, I walked a mindless path around the house, came back to the dining room, and let out a huge exhale. "Geez, Sylvie."

I slowly removed the box, setting it on the table. Inside was a purple velvet drawstring bag, but I couldn't bring myself to open it. My aunt, once a beautiful soul who'd walked this Earth, now fit inside that little bag. I held it close to my chest, thought about her dreams gone with the tide, then sobbed into my hands.

"Aunt Sylvie," I choked through tears. "You finally made it home."

Next evening, the full moon shone gloriously, the late July air was hot, and the wine flowed in another gorgeous moon party setup. This time, the design was my own. Using

Sylvie's inspiring collection of items, I'd set up a crystal-themed table, complete with huge amethyst quartz geode centerpieces, purple cloth napkins, crystals hanging from the tent fringes, and large pointy crystals rising up from each plate.

The wine goblets were tagged with little crystal rings at the base of the stems, and the napkin rings had all types of quartz—amethyst, rose, and citrine—attached to them. Even Heloise and Jeanine's white gauzy coverlets had crystals hanging off the edges. Also placed on the table were Sylvie's Tarot cards, Sylvie's mini crystal balls, and Sylvie's journals.

"Are these…"

"Sylvie's things, yes." I smiled.

"Oh, honey, I love it." Heloise clapped, delighted.

"Really lovely, Pulitzer." Jeanine hugged me. "And don't we look Stevie-Nicks-fabulous, darling?"

They both twirled in gauzy, matching caftans.

"You sure do. What about me?" I twirled, too, after mine finally arrived.

"A beautiful baby witch," Jeanine said. "But you're missing something."

"What's that?" I asked.

Out of her bag, she pulled my sun hat, now outfitted with a snazzy band of pink and yellow Lily Pulitzer fabric, tied into a bow. "For our new neighbor, Lily Blanchett."

"Jeanine, this is amazing! Thank you!" I tried on the hat. I knew I looked like Mrs. Roper from *Three's Company* but I didn't care. Mrs. Roper was one cool crone.

"I still had old scraps in a box from my aunt's factory days. Figured I'd put one to good use."

203

"Now, you see, guys? We'd never be able to do this again on an Atlantis-owned beach, would we?" I said.

"We would've found another place," Heloise said. "But no, nowhere like here. This is our magical corner of the universe. Thank you, Lily, for talking me off the ledge. Jeanine and I truly appreciate it."

"Yeah, thanks, Pulitzer. It hasn't been an easy week."

Heloise poured wine and lifted her glass. "To Aunt Sylvie. We miss you, old gal, but thank you from the bottom of our hearts for choosing us as your dearest friends. May you rest in joy and magic forever. As above, so below."

"Above, so below," Jeanine echoed.

"Above, so below," I said, because even though I wasn't a fully-fledged witch, it felt right. "To Aunt Sylvie." I raised my glass of pinot noir.

"To Aunt Sylvie!" Jeanine and Heloise toasted. We clinked glasses. "May she join us for every moon party from now on until the end of our moon partying days."

"May that be many, many years from now. Hear, hear," I said.

And the night of revelry began—the laughter, the wine, the delicious dinner I'd made, the abundance, the joy, the tears as the ladies told stories about Aunt Sylvie, and I shared mine from when I was a child. I cried over how I'd lost time getting to know her, and they consoled me.

"We got to know her for you," they said. "And boy, do we have stories."

"Like what? I need to hear more. All of them." I poured my second glass of wine. By this time, the twinkling lights were swaying, the ocean waves were crashing softly on the shore, and the bonfire roared high, sparking and crackling in a plume of embers.

"Let's start with Salty Sid," Heloise said.

"I knew it." I smiled.

"Boy, did those two know how to make their own bonfires on this beach," Jeanine said, lighting up a cigarette. "And they'd get loud."

Heloise giggled into my shoulder. "Oo, when that boy was getting close, you could hear, 'Oh, Sylvie! Oh, Sylvie!' all the way down the street." She roared with laughter, genuine tears in her sparkly eyes.

"That…is an image I did not need in my head." I hid my face in her shoulder.

"Yes, and he loved her, he did." Heloise wiped her tears of laughter away. "They were never an official couple, because your aunt didn't want a man or any relationship for a while, but whatever they had, it worked for them. When are you going to tell Sid about Sylvie, Lil?"

"Soon." I fell into another wave of sadness. "But tonight is a full moon. We're here to manifest our fullest potential, right? Our futures and what we want to achieve?"

"Yes, very good, fledgling! Do we all have our lists?" Jeanine stood and danced over to the bonfire. "We'll read them aloud and throw them into the flames of transmutation!" she said dramatically.

"Not throw them off a bridge this time?" I asked.

"Nay, the fire will transform our intentions into reality. Sends your message to the universe. Fire creates life, gives fuel to your dreams."

"I'm so ready for that." I skipped across the sand to the bonfire where Heloise began drumming a small drum, and we danced to the beat in a circle under the moonlight, humming our own tunes that somehow blended together as one.

We read aloud our lists, one by one, then threw the papers into the fire, raised our glasses again, and toasted underneath constellations aplenty. I asked for a successful new business venture, new friends, and for my talents to serve me for the rest of my life so I'd never again have to depend on a man.

Already, all three were coming true. I felt more powerful than ever, unstoppable, resilient. And like Jeanine said, I knew how to manifest like nobody's business. How I became a cottage witch who loved her island, I wasn't sure, but while these beautiful women had had a chance to experience that life for years, I was only just beginning.

"Ladies, ladies…" Heloise held onto my arm to keep from falling drunk on the sand. "I've reached a decision."

"About?" I muttered.

"The house. Let's stay and fulfill Sylvie's wish. Our wish. Jeanine, I love you. I'm sorry I put you through hell this week, honey, but mercury was retrograde, what can I say? Answers were muddy. I'm sorry."

"It's okay." Jeanine kissed Heloise on the lips. I hadn't seen them do that until now and felt happy that they were comfortable enough to do so with me present. We were all our best selves here tonight—together.

They kissed again, and I left them to it, dancing around the circle by myself, raising energy, putting the good vibes out there. I may have had hardly any money left in my bank account, but I had a house, I had Aunt Sylvie home again, I had a haunted cat, I had Bowie, my kids were doing well in college, and for the first time in a long, long time, I had friends. That was as good a place to start as any.

Spontaneously, I slipped off my hat and caftan and threw both onto the sand. Sliding off my undergarments, I struck a pose and announced my status as naked-under-a-full-moon-witch. "Ta-da!" I extended my arms.

"Ayyyy!"

When the ladies cheered, I was sure we could be heard cackling for miles down the beach, but I didn't care. Neither did they, as they joined me in beautiful, flabby, saggy, powerful "nudiness" and together, we frolicked and celebrated life around the fire.

Opening Aunt Sylvie's purple pouch, I lifted out a handful of sandy ashes and spread them in wild arcs of joy and gratitude over the beach, singing, laughing, and dancing, as waves ebbed, and air bubbles popped in the sand, logs crackled, and our bonfire transmuted, with love, my beautiful, generous, witchy aunt back into the universe.

21

If I was going to stay, there was much to do.

First, I had to return the rental car. I had to fly back to NYC to pack and send boxes down. I had to vacate the old house, maybe do another "letting go" ritual there, too. I had to sign paperwork for taking ownership of Sylvie's home. I had to tell the kids and my mom that I was moving to the Keys. I had to figure out where the next several months of income would come from.

Not gonna lie, I was still nervous not knowing where the money would come from, or how soon I'd make it without startup money for the B&B, but I wasn't going to worry about that now.

Like Heloise had told me, *You set the goal, work hard, and let the universe figure the rest out.* Having faith in the universe meant giving up control. Hard for me, but I was learning.

I'd put together a business plan, same way I'd done with *Chelsea Garden Grill* so many years ago. I'd take it to the bank and apply for a small business loan. My long-term goal was to buy other empty houses in the Keys and eventually convert those to B&Bs, too.

I thought about all this, as I painted the mermaid statue. For six weeks, she'd watched the insanity that was my life in silence, never judging, simply observing. I'd scoured Sylvie's photo albums trying to find photos of what she'd looked like before her paint flaked away, but then, it didn't matter. I'd paint her my way.

Intently, Bowie watched. Because Bowie was a connoisseur of fine art.

"Why are you giving me that look?" I asked the feline critic. "Mermaids' tails are teal blue. You wouldn't know. You're a land creature."

Bowie's one green, one blue eye blinked then settled at half-mast.

"Yes, I'm aware that I'm a land creature, too, but I have more experience in these matters than you do." Bowie blinked lazily. "I do, too. Now stop arguing with me."

My phone rang. Emily calling. Lately, my kids only called when they either needed money or wanted to file a complaint against their father, but at least they were calling.

"Hello, intelligent, powerful daughter," I answered in a cheery voice.

"Hi, Mom, have you checked your texts?"

Ugh, what now.

"Not since an hour ago. Why, what is it?" My stomach crunched onto itself. I put Emily on speaker while I checked my texts. Not from Emily, but from my old neighbor, Mrs. Napoli. Photos of Weasel moving stuff out of the house, sent in a group chat to me, Emily, and Chase (who'd marked the photo with the question mark emoji). "What is this?"

"It's Dad. He's an idiot!" Emily let out a frustrated scream. "Remember the day I found him inside the house, I called you to tell you about it?"

"Yes?"

"Those photos are from that day. Mrs. Napoli took pics of him going in and out of the house. What the heck is her problem?"

"I don't know, but she shouldn't be sending them in a group text involving my children," I muttered, anger I'd suppressed working its way up my chest. More than ever, I wanted this garbage over so I could move on with life.

Emily scoffed. "The point is that he was taking stuff, and not just shirts and underwear either. Why would he need your computer? Mom, he only ever used his laptop and iPad. You're the one who used that computer for business. You need to call him and put him on blast."

"My guess is he's probably looking for evidence of...I don't know...anything he can use against me. Records of funds, purchases I made, loans I took out. Who the hell knows, but you're right, those are mine."

What else had he gone through that day? Was he hoping to find evidence of extramarital affairs? Any search would come out dry. I never so much as talked to another man during our marriage.

Unless he used my computer for other things I didn't know about. As if I'd use that against him. He'd already done enough damage.

"I understand he's keeping the restaurant, so he might need records," Emily said, "but why does he have to be so shady about it? Why can't he just ask *you* for the documents he needs instead of breaking into the house and taking it, like a criminal."

I wanted to take my daughter and hold her close. "I know how you feel, Em. This is what divorce does to people. It makes them enemies of war. It didn't have to be this way, and it won't always be this way, I promise."

210

"I don't even know him anymore, Mom."

"Me neither. But remember, he could be following his lawyer's advice, or his new girlfriend's, or any number of new people in his life. The point is, we have to leave him be. Sure, he's making one blunder after another, but we can't stand in his way."

"You're saying we have to stand back and watch him become a train wreck?"

"Basically. We can't control him. All we can do is control how we react. I'm sorry, Emily. I hope that once things settle down after the divorce, you can start your relationship with your dad over again."

"I doubt it. He's shattered everything I thought I knew about him."

That made two of us, three if we included Chase. I had to believe that once things settled down, however, Weasel would try and reestablish his relationship with his kids. I couldn't stand the thought of them losing him completely to a new family.

We talked another minute, then I sent Emily on her way, thinking more positive thoughts when all I'd really done was absorb her anguish and make it my own, so she could feel better. I sat under the sun, trembling, thinking of the million things I wanted to tell Derek, debating whether or not I should call him.

The mermaid watched me. *Don't,* she seemed to say. *It doesn't matter. Whatever he wants to take, let him. There is nothing there you need anymore.*

It was true.

Myself? Had it.

My kids? Had them.

My future goals? Here, with me.

211

Nothing I needed remained in Long Island. The mermaid was pretty wise, let me tell you. However, something told me I needed to end this. Bullies took as long as they were allowed to, and Derek had become a bully. I couldn't let go without letting him know he couldn't take advantage of me.

Rather than call, I texted him the photos.

Got all the evidence you needed?

It took him a few minutes to reply while I painted scales on the mermaid's tail, but finally...

*You don't need the restaurant
files anymore.*

*I don't care what you think
I need or don't need, Derek.
Until the divorce is final and
a court orders me to hand
over the papers, you don't
come into the house.
You hear me?*

The house is mine, Lily.

*I have a restraining order
against you, Derek.*

A bullshit one, but you

weren't home, so it doesn't matter.

It matters. You aren't allowed within a hundred feet of the property. Isn't that funny? You can't come near your own house. Ah, the irony. In a minute, I'm calling the police to have you arrested for breaking your restraining order. I just thought you'd want to make sure you're dressed before they show up.

Screw off.

Gladly. You've already taken everything you can from me when I didn't do anything to deserve this. I don't care how cold you think I was to you when we were together, I don't deserve this. A decent man would at least let me keep the house for his kids to live in. Though I still have that chance after you're arrested, actually.

I haven't taken anything compared to you keeping the kids from me.

Really? He thought I was keeping the kids from him? Was that what all this was about? What a maroon.

That has nothing to do with me. I've spent a year defending you when I have no reason to. That's how much I don't want them to lose hope. But you, you're doing a fine job of keeping the kids away from you ALL ON YOUR OWN. Don't text back. I'm done.

Tears sat, hot and fresh, on my lids, but I wouldn't let him have the satisfaction. He did not get to ruin my life with any more of his lies. I stopped texting but before I could read his reply and risk the urge to reply yet again, I threw the phone over the fence, myself this time. Onto the beach where it couldn't suck me in again.

Then I got back to work on the mermaid. That Mona Lisa smile was there again. *Good job, Lil. Proud of you.*

That night, during a dinner of roasted chicken (poultry for the first time after eight weeks of gorging on seafood), I consumed Sylvie's journal cover to cover in search of anything that could help me. Heloise explained it was called a Book of Shadows or grimoire, a record containing all her instructions for spells and rituals she'd done herself. I kept the leather-bound book open between two candles. Until now, I'd used magic to help take me to the next phase of life but not to affect others.

Tonight, that would change.

I found something that might prove useful, something called a "Let Him Go Binding Spell," to be performed during a waning moon. Why did Sylvie have this?

"Perfect," I told Bowie.

He agreed but wanted more chicken to be sure. He also wanted to know who Aunt Sylvie had needed to bind.

"Good question. It couldn't be Sid. He's such a nice guy." Then, I remembered the empty spots in her photo album where certain images had been clearly removed. "Aunt Sylvie, you were hurt, too, weren't you?"

The instructions called for finding a photo of the person whose actions I wanted to bind, tie a palm frond around it with a tight knot, and utter the words, *I bind you, Derek, from doing any more harm against others. Stay away from me. I will no longer let you hurt me.*

I searched the house for a photo of Derek but considering this hadn't been my home for very long, I didn't have a print of him anywhere. The only one I'd had was in my wallet, but I'd long taken it out. Maybe I could pull up an image from the internet then bind my phone? Nah, my phone had been through enough damage.

I texted Jax.

Do you have a printer?

I do. It's big. And can handle anything. What are you wearing?

I had to laugh. Because Jax.

*Could I come over for a second
to print something and you
promise you won't ask any questions?*

*Sounds hot. Will I get
arrested for helping?*

Possibly.

I'm in.

I turned around so fast, my foot caught inside the box of old mail Sid brought me that'd been pushed up against the wall, or so I thought. A quarter of the bills spilled onto the floor, and I hit my knee against the floor. "Ouch. Stupid...box." I started collecting them when I noticed a personal letter tucked in between the bills, coupons, and other spam.

It was addressed to Sylvie but had no return address except for a hand drawing of a boat in the upper left corner. Nervous about opening mail that wasn't mine, I set it down, told myself it wasn't my business, then reminded myself it was, because Sylvie had gone to the Great Beyond, and I was the new house owner.

I sighed and opened the letter.

It was from Sid. A short and sweet, one-page letter telling her how much he enjoyed the time they'd spent together on and off over the years, that he respected the distance she'd asked for, but that he knew it was only because of some guy named Todd that she was scared to be with anyone else. Todd had so stomped on her heart, it had closed her off to love. However, if she ever felt the courage to take love on again, she knew where to find him.

Signed—Sid

I set the letter down and stared into space.

The letter was marked thirteen years ago, the same year Sylvie left her home forever for assisted care in Tampa. She and Sid had to be in their 50s and 60s at the time of whatever they had together, which told me one thing—love and romance was still possible at that age.

There I'd been, thinking my life was over after Derek left, but it was only just beginning, like Salty Sid said the first time I met him. Sid and Sylvie, even though they didn't stay together, still gave me hope that new adventures awaited me.

"Thanks, guys," I said, then hobbled over to Jax's in my bare feet, braless again, because: Florida Keys. But also, because: I wanted Jax to see.

I knocked. He answered in shorts, shirtless again, flip flops. Would Jax be my Sid? Would we have lots of adventures to come if I stayed? Would we remain friends or find love? In the background, I saw he was working on his website. That sent a twinge of pride through me.

"Hey! Sorry to bother you."

His smile stretched from ear to ear, his eyes flitting to my chest then back up. "Do I look like I'm bothered?"

I tried to not stare at *his* chest, which just happened to be at eye level. *Soon, maybe,* I reminded myself. "I'm guessing your printer is the *Brother* that just came up and your Wi-Fi is 'SeaWitch81?'"

"That would be the one."

I fired off the photo of Weasel and heard machinery whir in the background. Jax went to get the print. "I'm actually designing my website. It's really easy, like you said. Are you proud of me?"

"Incredibly. And *I* threw my phone over the fence today so I wouldn't get into another text war with Derek. You proud of me?"

"Nice! Looks like we're both getting bad habits out of our sys—" He paused, looked at the photo of Derek in his hands. "Maybe not."

"Like I said, no questions asked." I smiled, took the sheet from Jax, and backed away, twiddling my fingers. "Thanks, I owe you."

"No problem. Oh, and hey…"

I turned at the sidewalk. "Yeah?"

"When you fold that sheet," he said, "make sure to bend it away from you, like you're getting rid of him. Not towards you. That brings the energy back. Got it?" He pressed his smile into a knowing smirk, then closed the door.

All I could do was process.

He knew. Jax knew what I was doing. He knew about binding spells and magickal things, but of course he did. He had a boat named *Sea Witch*, after his mother Aurelia who'd helped others find peace using bottles of the ocean's moods. He had a natural spark in his eye and an affinity for nature.

Son of a witch, I thought.

I jogged back to the house, grabbed a bowl, matches, and took Sylvie's grimoire out to the sand in search of a fallen palm frond. Finding a small one, I tore one leaf and proceeded with the binding spell.

"I bind you, Derek Blanchett, from doing any more harm against others. Stay away from me. I will no longer let you hurt me."

I folded the photo *away*, like Jax had said, then tied it with the frond, imagining Derek ceasing his harm. With my eyes closed, I imagined him ending his reign of pain. For good measure, because this spell was for stopping what I no longer wanted, I imagined him ceasing his awkward estrangement from the kids as well.

I struck a match, lit the corner of the paper bundle on fire and let it burn inside the bowl until there was nothing left but a pile of black ashes. I sat a while, imagining all harm coming to an end, all of us moving on with our lives.

Sylvie's instructions then said to take the ashes and bury them in the sand off-property, so I went for a walk. Down the beach, a quarter mile south, enjoying the stars and waning moon winking in the sky, feeling more and more in control with each step. When I'd passed four other houses at the end of four other streets, I came to the edge of the rocks and, crouching low to dig a hole in the sand, dumped the ashes then recovered them with wet sand.

"You will no longer hurt me, Derek Blanchett," I said loudly. "I take back my power!"

The quiet waves lapped against the shore.

The universe smiled, and a salty sailor said, "Nice work."

22

"Sid?"

He waved from a lounge chair on a rickety houseboat tethered to a nearby dock. "Sorry. Wasn't trying to spy on ya or anything, but you were shouting."

"I...I was..."

"I know. No need to explain," he called back.

I walked all the way to the dock and climbed on, the slosh of water underneath me. Sid met me halfway holding a bag of mussels. "Want these? They'll go bad soon if someone doesn't take them."

"Sure, I can make something with them. Hey, uh, I'm glad I found you here. I have some news you should know. I should've told you sooner."

"About Sylvie?"

"Yes. She's gone, Sid. She passed away last week. I'm sorry. I know you two were friends."

He dropped his chin and nodded. He looked so sad, I had to lean in and give him a hug. "That we were, Lily," he said, patting my back. "That we were. I knew this day would come, but we're never ready, are we?"

"No, we're not." I pulled away. "And I also want you to know something, 'cause otherwise it's just going to eat away at my conscience, but um…I saw the letter you sent my aunt inside the box of mail you gave me."

"Oh?" He lifted the edge of his collar to blot his eyes.

"Yeah." I wrung my hands together. "You sent it a while back. You thanked her for the time you spent together and said if it hadn't been for Todd, the two of you might've been able to be more."

"Oh, that."

"Who was Todd?"

"Todd lived with her for a short time, a few months maybe. Years ago. Fella was from Boston or someplace, had money, made her lots of shiny promises, like helping her open her bed-and-breakfast. She was in love with him, but any of us could see he wasn't in it for the long run. Then one day, he just up and left. She was hurt real bad. Closed her off to trying again."

"I had no idea," I said. Not a surprise, considering how little I knew about my aunt.

"Heloise said that Annie probably spooked him because she didn't like him, and I'll tell you Annie don't spook nobody she doesn't like."

"She must've known he was a bad egg."

"That's what I say." Sid smacked his lips. "Aw, it don't matter anyway. I was lucky enough to be in Sylvie's life as long as I was. No regrets. You, you bring joy back to that house, Lily." Sparkly blue eyes winked. "That's enough for me."

Salty Sid then turned and headed back to his houseboat, whistling a sailor tune.

With all her new details, the mermaid was coming back to life, too. Though I wasn't finished, she was already making the garden look magical again. I just needed to add highlights to her brown hair, sparkles to her scales, and shading to her skin. Last, I would cover her in a clear coat then post my masterpiece on social media for all to see.

It was, however, a scorcher of a day, which delayed things. I lifted my sun hat, brushed the sweat off my forehead, and was about to grab a few key limes to make refreshing limeade when my phone rang.

Carmen again. I braced.

Whatever it is, you can handle it, I told myself. "Hey, has anyone told you you're amazing today? Well, you are."

She giggled. Whew. "Hi, Lily. How the heck are ya?"

"Let's see, I live on the beach, there's coconut palms in my backyard, I'm friends with a mermaid and two witches, I get cheap, fresh seafood delivered to my back door, and my neighbor is a half-Cuban GQ model-slash-boat captain. How does that sound to you?" I made my way into the kitchen.

"Dreamy, honestly. I wish I could join you."

"Why don't you?" I sliced two of the limes. "Just come down for a little. You can be my first guest when I open. Or you can come now and help me get things ready."

"You're really doing it, huh? You're going to stay?"

"I am, Carmen. It's weird, I know. I never expected to fall in love with this place. I guess I had to get away from all the noise."

"New York hurt you, didn't it?"

"I wouldn't say that. NYC was good to me, and I do miss the hectic energy some days. I miss the kids. I miss you. But if I can get you and the kids down here for a visit, then problem solved." Adding water, sugar, and ice, I stirred it all up and took a huge chug.

Ah, the simple things.

"You sound happy, Lil. That's a big improvement from the last time we talked."

"Hey. I don't want to jinx anything, but I think I'm coming out of the dark. I woke up this morning feeling different. I honestly believe the worst may be over. That might be naïve since the divorce isn't over yet, I still have to sign the marital settlement agreement, but it's where I am."

"I'm glad to hear that, because I'm calling to tell you something. I hope you won't get mad—it's a good thing."

"Uh, oh, what happened?" So much for hoping Carmen hadn't called to give me any distressing news.

"Remember how you told me about the bed-and-breakfast idea and possibly fusing your Halloween-themed future restaurant with your new digs, how it could work?"

"Oh, Carmen, what did you do?"

"I told Dade about it."

"Of course, you did."

"Well, we are living with each other temporarily, Lily, and it just sort of slipped out in conversation. I was talking about how or where I would find a job and start over, then I mentioned you and how you were kicking ass down in the Keys, taking names, owning your truth, and well…"

"Go ahead…"

"He loved it. People love how you responded to Derek's cheating, Lil."

"They do? I thought they all assumed I was nuts."

"Well, they do, but in a good way. When you burned his stuff on the sidewalk, you spoke for legions of fed-up women."

"I did? I haven't been online in a long time. I wasn't sure what people were saying. Honestly, I was trying not to find out."

"You're like an icon now. I'm in awe of you."

"Aww, thanks." Considering I was thirteen years older than she was, I took that as a compliment. Guess there were good things to be taken from this experience. "So how is any of this bad?"

"It's not, but Dade took it upstairs."

"To the senior execs, you mean."

"Yes, and…"

"And?"

"Everyone agreed you would make an amazing host for a new food show, kind of like No Reservations meets Christine McConnell, except you don't travel but you do host a B&B."

"And I don't have an eighteen-inch waist."

"Who cares? You would make the most gorgeous spooky hostess. Long story short, they've been throwing the idea around, and…well, I wasn't supposed to say anything, but damn it, Lil, we've been friends longer than I've been dating Dade."

Sucking in a breath, I sat in the grass and thought about how I would have liked to pitch this idea myself, so I could be involved from the start. *However*, sometimes life threw you fastballs, and you had to roll with the punches, or some applicable sports metaphor anyway.

"So, you decided to tell me what they're up to, even if the idea doesn't go anywhere, just so I'm aware?"

"Basically."

"Thank you."

"But not really. There's more."

"Girl, you're killing me."

Carmen giggled. "*Cooking Network* execs apparently pitched it to Elaine Driver and Josh Schubert who just happened to be in Miami for the International Summer in the Sun Festival, and well…"

Elaine and Josh, the owners of the network, had already heard my half-baked idea casually brought up in conversation to my ex-restaurant's ex-manager to her junior exec boyfriend? Oh, boy. "They want me to drive up to talk?"

"They're coming to you."

"What?!" I stood so fast, I lost my balance and staggered into the mermaid, knocking her off her base a few inches.

"They're on their way to you now, I think. Oh, God, you're mad, aren't you?"

"No, I'm…trying to keep a statue from falling. Hold on." I tossed the phone into the grass and used both hands to lean the mermaid against the wooden fence, which groaned under the weight. "Crap, crap…" The square base on which she sat was also askew. I never knew any of these pieces were mobile.

I squatted to pick up the phone, the wind knocked out of me. "So, what you are saying is you accidentally spilled my beans, inadvertently setting a snowball in motion, and now I need to go get dressed as quickly as possible, because the network is surprise-visiting me any minute now to discuss my undeveloped idea before the snowball becomes an avalanche."

"Something like that."

"Got it."

"Do you hate me?"

"Carmen Figueras, I will never hate you. We may have been co-workers for fifteen years, but you have become my dearest friend, and as of late, my only friend from my old life. I love you."

"Aww, Lily. I love you, too. I swear I didn't mean for this to happen, but it's a good thing, isn't it?" From the trepidation in her voice, it was clear she really needed my forgiveness.

"It is. And this isn't my first rodeo with the execs. Let me go get ready. I'll call you back once they leave, okay? Do not fret over this another minute."

We hung up, and I stood in the lush garden, at a crossroads, not knowing where to turn next. *Cooking Network* folks were already on their way, but the statue was heavily leaning against a rickety fence, and I didn't want to risk it falling and breaking. Neither Annie nor Sylvie would like that. I wouldn't be too happy about it either.

I texted Jax to see if he was available. Within seconds, I heard his front porch screen door open and slap shut and a knock at my front door.

"I'm in the garden!" I shouted.

He entered the house and emerged through my side door, holding an inverted slice of mango. "Wa smm?" He held it out to me.

"Maybe later."

"Picked up too many from my aunt. You can make something with them. Mango ice cream, mango salsa, mango shakes… Whoa, what did she do to you?" Jax eyed the knocked-over mermaid.

"It was an accident. Can you help me put her back?" I tried lifting her off the fence and noticed a hairline fracture on her neck. "Shit, I think she's cracked."

"Hold on, hold on…" Jax rushed over and helped me lift her carefully off the wooden planks and into position when I pointed out the square stone base beneath her had also moved. "We're going to have to lie her down. Carefully, so we don't snap the water tube. Looks brittle. Ready?"

"Alright, one sec. Ready."

"Towards me on one, two…"

"Go."

On three, we lay her down in the grass, exposing the small, rusted motor underneath, the electrical cord buried in the foliage all the way to the house, and something else. The concrete base was about twenty-by-twenty inches and bolted into a slightly smaller, but thick, piece of wood underneath.

Jax squatted to examine it. "Wood looks half-rotten. I think we should take it out. I can replace it with a new plank."

"I'll buy it, but it'll have to be later. Right now, I have to get ready for visitors on their way. Thanks for helping. You around later? I wanted to talk to you."

"Hold on, Lil…" He picked at the wood, lifting the splintered, chafed corners, and tossing them aside. "Does this look like a base to you?"

I pointed at the edges with my toes. "This part looks like a frame, almost."

"Right? Like an attic door. See, there's this space going all around. This almost looks like…" Digging his fingers into the narrow space, barely making them in, he bit down on his bottom lip, and turning red and sweaty, lifted the corner of the large piece of square plywood. "It's nailed. Be right back."

He literally jogged off in a hurry, while I sat there examining the odd wooden base, the mermaid staring at me amusedly from her prone position in the grass.

"You knew this was here, didn't you?"

She smiled without comment.

"What are you hiding, little lady?"

Jax returned with a crowbar and eagerness in his eyes. He wedged the end of it into the space, prying the edge of the wood up, exposing two to three rusted old nails on each of the four sides. "Stand back." He positioned his sandaled foot and knee in a way to gain leverage. Then, with a grunt, he pried the whole door open on three sides. Flipping the one, still-attached piece on its side, we stood back.

It was hard to know what hit me first, the stanky plume of humidity into my nostrils or the realization that a set of stairs were leading down into darkness. "No. Freakin. Way." My mouth fell agape, and my heart beat a thousand miles per second. "Did you know this was here?"

Jax shook his head, slowly looking at me, then back at the hatch we'd just opened. "Nuh, uh."

"How long has this fountain been here?" I asked. "Before Sylvie, or after?"

"It was here when I played in her yard as a kid, so I'm guessing it's been here longer than that," Jax said.

"We'll have to check old photos."

"Alright, who's going in first?" He tapped the flashlight on his phone and turned the camera on. "It's your house. But if you don't want to, I can go first."

"Let's both go in," I said. "You first, and if you say it's okay, I'll follow." I felt like Indiana Jones discovering the lost Ark, except this had been under my nose—our noses—the whole time. "I'm guessing your house doesn't have something like this? Like, it's not a feature of the homes built here, is it?"

"Mine and Heloise's houses were built long after Annie's. She lived alone on this street for many years. Before there was even a street, most likely. Probably from the twenties through the fifties."

"Do you think it's a bomb shelter?" I hated to say it, but back in the sixties, lots of homes had these, especially when nuclear threat was real, given the island's proximity to Guantanamo.

"I don't know, Lil. I'm going in. If anything happens to me, tell my kid I loved him." He said this so seriously, it broke my heart. He handed me his phone. "Keep the camera rolling."

"Nothing's going to happen. Geez, Jax, this is exciting."

"Snakes." He tossed a length of sea grass that had grown between the steps up into my face. "Why'd it have to be snakes?"

"Careful." I illuminated his path. Those steps looked like they could give out at any moment, but he made it down about ten feet then stood on solid ground just fine.

He reached up his hand. "My phone, please, then come down carefully. The first few steps are wet. Actually, this whole floor is slimy."

Made sense. The wooden hatch door had nothing to seal it against the elements of ocean water and South Florida rainstorms. Even with a mermaid sitting on top of it, some was going to leak through. I handed Jax his phone then turned, so I could descend while still holding onto the stairs with both hands.

"What the…" Jax mumbled.

"Wait for me." When my feet touched the floor, and things felt solid and real, I let go of the railing. The flashlight wasn't necessary. Enough sunlight streamed in to show us what was there.

Holy…

A room—a large room, about twenty-by-twenty feet, laced with cobwebs, wooden walls and floor, full of shelves, dark brown bottles with labels on them, oak barrels, the kinds you see in wineries or cartoons with people going down Niagara Falls, copper kettle containers, tubes leading into one of them, and…was that a vintage record player?

A Victrola?

The music I sometimes heard playing late at night?

"Jax, it can't be. Am I really seeing this?" I went up to the antique player and blew off a layer of dust that flew into the stagnant air and hung there, suspended.

"You are. It's her distillery." He gripped my arm, as I held onto his. "It's Annie Jackson's distillery, Lily."

"It's Annie Jackson's distillery," I repeated.

"It's Annie Jackson's distillery!" we cried together, clasping hands.

"Guys, whoever is watching this, this is amazing. A discovery right in our own backyard," I said into the camera. "This is unbelievable. I bet this is what I could see from the beach."

I bet this was what Annie herself had been pointing to on the night she materialized, too.

"From outside?" Jax asked.

"Yes, a few feet behind my house, it looks like a boardwalk, wooden planks hiding under the sand," I explained. "I always thought it was a bike path that had gotten covered over time."

"How did I never see this?" Jax wondered.

"How did my aunt never see this?"

We knew nothing. Only that life was filled with mystery and awe-inspiring moments, and if we gave up on life, we'd miss them.

I peered into one of the dark shelves. "Old Annie's Registered Brand Whiskey, Bottled in Bond at Distillery, Skeleton Key, FL." The date said 1931 on the entire row of whiskey. On the shelf underneath it, a similar label except darker sepia toned displayed Old Annie's Registered Brand Rum. "This one is rum. I can't believe this. Jax, this is…"

There had to be about sixty to seventy bottles of aged liquor in here.

Jax grabbed fistfuls of his hair. "This is crazy. We have to tell the others. We have to—"

"I'll do the telling. It's my aunt's house."

"Yes, totally." He paced nervously in a circle.

"Do not post that video. I have guests about to arrive. We have to close this up for now and come back later."

"Okay…"

Except we couldn't. We kept walking around, picking up and examining bottles of rum and whiskey, and even a few of wine, all with Old Annie's label on them. Perfectly sealed with wax, perfectly preserved in time. Ninety years of these items just sitting here waiting to be discovered. On a spacious counter, old, yellowed paper sat underneath a few tools, along with large mixing spoons and a glass jug. Ingredient measurements scrawled in pencil, in Annie's very own handwriting.

"Look at this." I pointed.

Jax peered at the paper, hands behind his back. Neither of us wanted to touch anything else with our dirt-encrusted hands for fear of tarnishing the treasure.

"You have to call the state, Lil. These bottles could be worth up to a thousand each, I'll bet. Maybe even more, since she was a pretty famous person down here. I'm blown away. Look at me, I'm in tears."

Indeed, he was, as was I.

We hugged and danced a little jig. This was, hands down, the most amazing thing to happen to me since the birth of my children. Had I not taken my mom's advice, I'd still be in Long Island, still holding onto a life that no longer existed, still angry, still trying to find my way.

Thanks, Mom.

The moment I accepted the universe's challenge, everything started opening up to me. Even the floor had opened up, proving that life's mysteries were hidden in every corner, sometimes underneath our very own feet.

We took photos—lots of them—full shots and close-ups, and videos, too. But the minute Jax and I crammed into the frame together, cheek to cheek, for a selfie, we turned to each other—ecstatic, sweaty, not giving a shit, and we kissed. Hot, urgent, impatiently.

Why had we waited so long?

Scratch that—I knew. But I was done waiting. I wanted this, and so did he, and there was nothing, *nothing* wrong with that. This was the moment. He'd been there for me all these weeks, my friend with and without benefits, and now I wanted to express my thanks.

The moment our kissing sent us bumping into Annie's shelves and catching wobbling bottles before they fell was the moment we flew out of the distillery, hand in hand, laughing as we slipped in the slime, straight upstairs, straight for the shower, straight for the steam and heat.

And yeah—straight for sex magic.

After Jax went home, I sat downstairs in the dining room, peeking out the window, ridiculous smile on my face. No matter what Elaine and Josh had to say about the TV show idea, as far as I was concerned, my day had already been made. I'd found Annie Jackson's distillery, made love with the gorgeous Captain Jax, and everything seemed to be falling into place.

The car rolled up, and I went out to greet them.

Elaine and Josh, hopeful expressions on their faces, waved hello. "Lily! Is this a good time? Sorry to drop in like this, but we're in town only a few more hours."

Behind them, prouder than a peacock, was my little Luna. I knew who she really was. Somehow, I'd always known—she was Annie, watching over her home and all who lived in it.

I smiled. She winked her gorgeous golden eyes and vanished. "A perfect time. Come on in, guys."

23

A lot can happen in eight months.

I know, because I was standing in my completely remodeled black, green, and chrome kitchen, decorated with cobwebs, witches' brooms, whiskey bottles, distillery equipment, cauldrons, and more. A makeup artist was finishing off my eyebrows, and a hair stylist was putting the last touches on my Veronica Lake hairdo.

I watched the hubbub unfold. Camera crews, booms, mics, set designers, our director, and Heloise and Jeanine, who I'd hired as kitchen assistants, all shuffled around me in slow motion.

"Where do you want this, Lily?" A designer held up one of my new skull soup bowls I'd had custom made from an artisan on Etsy.

"The hutch over there." I pointed to the new armoire in my 19th century Floridian-Victorian dining room, all set up and ready for my first guests to arrive, the excitement to be captured on camera in a reality TV-style food and lifestyle show.

Rather than dress me as a witch, the crew had agreed on giving me a classic pinup look, with a hibiscus bloom in my hair giving me a tropical flair. I went over my lines for the opening several more times, but I couldn't help but take it all in. The smiles, the energy, the excitement.

In early June, I was lost. A doormat, sad and afraid for my future. Now, I was the star of my own show, *The Witch of Key Lime Lane,* and the owner of my very own bed-and-breakfast on Skeleton Key. Heloise and Jeanine helped me prep for the first episode and would be assisting in the kitchen for the foreseeable future, while Jax and Sid agreed to appear on a few episodes as my boat captain and seafood selling neighbors.

My parents were here, getting a tour of the house, garden, and distillery by Emily and Chase, who'd come to visit twice since hearing the news I was staying. Jax's son, Brandon, was here, too. His friends were finally old enough to leave home for a weekend or two a month to hang at "Brandon's dad's house in the Keys," go on fishing trips, and be goofy seventeen-year-old boys. Overnight, he'd become the "cool" parent, and I didn't want to take credit or say that a little witchy magic had anything to do with that, because Jax *was* cool, but I may or may not have practiced my new craft on him.

A witch never tells.

On the home front, carpenters, painters, and craftsmen had worked to remodel Sylvie's place over the last six months, and now, rather than an outdated little Victorian, Aunt Sylvie's was a gingerbread-style beach cottage. The stuff of witchy aesthetic dreams! Not long after finding Annie's distillery under my house, Derek's lawyer announced his change to let me keep the house, but only if I agreed not to press charges on him for breaking and entering.

I took the deal, and the divorce was finally over.

The equity from the sale put cash into my account to fix up this house, not to mention the $2.5M the network was paying to play my life out in front of the cameras for twelve episodes.

The residents of Skeleton Key and I reported Annie's distillery to the State of Florida for its historical value, but because the items were less than 100 years old (just barely), we didn't have to hand anything over. We got to keep everything. However, I didn't want to sell her bottles. Annie's treasures should be shared with the world, so I applied for Florida Heritage Landmark status, and just two days ago, a State Historic Preservation Officer came to officially deem the garden and distillery a historic place, and they even installed the famous dark brown sign.

It was fun to see everyone taking pictures with my mermaid fountain, now fully functional in a spot next to the distillery entrance. Her smile was that of a siren finally awarded a great number of admirers.

The officers also determined that at least four other houses on the island might be considered for the Florida Heritage Landmark status—one used as a bordello in the 1800s, another as a Cuban cigar factory in the 1950s, another as a risqué dance theater from the 1930s, and another as an environmentalist conservatory in the 1950s, one that John Audubon had visited on a couple occasions.

I intended to buy them all one day.

Nobody could touch Skeleton Key—not a cruise line, not land developers, nobody but us homeowners.

Not everyone was happy we'd collectively turned down Atlantis Cruise Line, but the few who hated the decision sold their homes to private buyers anyway. Those who remained received a nice cash bonus from the network as a thanks for letting them tape on the island and were, for the most part, excited about the new show highlighting their neighborhood.

As Nanette said, "That'll make our homes even more valuable later on, so break a leg, Lily!"

Jeanine scooted into my view to show me the perfect key lime pie she'd made for the welcome spread. "What do you think?"

"Perfection," I replied. Before she could scuttle off, I grabbed her elbow. "Hey. I wanted to say thank you." Heloise hurried past, so I reined her in as well. "You, too."

"What's this? A coven meeting? Now? In front of everybody?"

"Pulitzer is getting mushy on us," Jeanine said.

"I just wanted to say thank you—to both of you. For letting me stay at your place for five months while they renovated. For teaching me your wise woman ways. For helping me make a new life for myself."

"For forcing you to listen to Fleetwood Mac every day?" Jeanine said.

"Yes, all of it." I smiled.

"We figured it was the only way to get free food from a celebrity chef for the rest of our natural lives, so really, it was all a ruse."

"So, you took advantage of me?"

"Yes." They both nodded.

"So proud of you. But seriously, you guys mean everything to me. Not just because of the moon parties, or the sage advice, or because you've taught me everything I know about manifesting, but because you were there for me. When I needed you most. That hadn't really hit me until just now." I fanned my eyes to prevent makeup from running. "Here I go."

All day, I'd been getting emotional.

Stupid estrogen.

"That's the universe at play, Pulitzer." Jeanine winked.

"Maybe. But thank *you* anyway. I'm thrilled I get to share this day with you." I hugged them, careful not to squish the pie between us. "That goes on the dining table with the rest of the stuff. Someone will probably move it around but let them. That's their job."

"I don't know about you," Heloise said to Jeanine, "but I love seeing this take-no-crap boss lady side of Lily."

"Right? She's intimidating, if I'm being honest." Jeanine gave me a faux scared look and shuffled away with the pie.

"How are we doing on time?" Kevin, the director, called.

Several shouts called back. "Ready when you are."

"Lily?"

"I'm ready."

Kevin made an announcement and reminder for anyone not actively participating in the shoot to please go wait behind the barricades in the street. There, they were welcome to take as many photos and videos as they liked, but not to post them, according to their contracts.

I watched as dozens of people filtered out of Sylvie's house—my house—my parents, my children, Salty Sid, Jax, Brandon and his buddies, all giving me waves and airy high fives from a distance.

Even though I'd done TV shows before, this felt a world different. This show was mine. I was not only the business brains of my own bed-and-breakfast, I was also the show's face—its star. Never could I have imagined a comeback last June. Now in February, my first guests awaited in a car with black tinted windows in front of Jax's house for their cue to come out.

Carmen Figueras had left *Chelsea Garden Grill* without knowing where to go. Turned out her boyfriend, Dade, had already been on the verge of asking her to live with him, and though she didn't know it yet—he'd be proposing this weekend. Both would be my first guests, and I couldn't wait to show them everything wonderfully magickal about Skeleton Key.

"Quiet on the set," Kevin called. "Lily, you ready?"

"As I'll ever be." I stood on the masking tape X on my creepy front porch, taking the deepest of breaths. An assistant carried Bowie over to me, all cleaned and fluffed and decked out in a lime green bow. My adorable co-host familiar. "Ready, Bo?"

"Places, everybody. Let's go for a first take on the intro. In three…two…"

The *one* was silent.

My smile felt serene. I looked into the camera swooping up the steps. "Hi, I'm Lily Autumn, restauranteur and owner of this beautiful witchy bed-and-breakfast in the Florida Keys, and this is my story."

The camera got a shot of Bowie, then I put him down on a gorgeous rattan chair, grabbed Sylvie's wooden sign, painted with our logo of a moon and cat, and walked it over to the hooks hanging off the front eaves. There, with great pride and joy, I hung my new, hand-painted sign…

GABRIELLE KEYES

AUTHENTIC KEY LIME PIE

16	graham crackers (the whole sheet = 1 cracker)
3 Tbsp.	sugar
¼ lb.	unsalted butter, softened
4	egg yolks
14 oz.	sweetened condensed milk
½ c.	fresh key lime juice
2 tsp.	key lime peel, grated
½ c.	heavy whipping cream
2 tsp.	sugar
¼ tsp.	pure vanilla extract

For the crust:
Preheat oven to 350° F. Process graham crackers, 3 Tbsp. sugar, and unsalted butter together in a food processor. Add more butter, if necessary, to make the mixture clump together. Press evenly into 9-inch pie plate. Bake for 10-12 minutes or until lightly browned. Remove from oven and cool on rack.

For the filling:
Using whip attachment, beat egg yolks on medium speed until thick and yellow. Turn mixer off and add sweetened condensed milk. Turn mixer to low. Add ½ the key lime juice. Once mixed, add the other half and the zest. Mix again on low. Pour mixture into cooled pie shell and bake at 350° for 12 minutes. Remove from oven and cool to room temperature, then transfer to refrigerator for 3+ hours.

For topping:
In cold, stainless steel bowl, add heavy whipping cream, 2 tsp. sugar, and vanilla extract. Whip with whip attachment until stiff peaks form. Pipe border onto refrigerated key lime pie, or dollop onto each slice when served.

P.S. An authentic key lime pie always has a graham cracker crust, whipped cream (not meringue), and is never, ever green! Enjoy. :) - Gabrielle Keyes

WITCH OF KEY LIME LANE

Book #2 in the *Dead & Breakfast* Series

CRONE OF COCONUT COURT

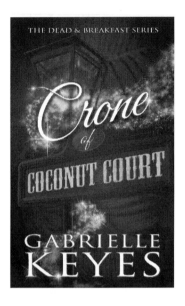

A middle-aged woman at rock bottom. An ex who took it all. An old Victorian cottage awaiting new life.

For 22 years, Katja Miller was a good wife to her husband, an excellent mother to two daughters (now in college), and a volunteer at her church's community bookshop. But even in a small Midwestern town, life throws you curveballs. So, when her ex takes off with another woman, leaving nothing but $68 in their account, Katja must figure out where to go from here.

Watching a show called *Witch of Key Lime Lane*, Katja takes her biggest risk ever and applies for a temporary job as assistant to TV's gothic goddess, Lily Autumn. Never imagining to actually get hired, Katja finally leaves Hendersonville for a place in Florida called Skeleton Key.

But the old house on the beach is a creepy place where locked trunks open at will, dolls show up in the most random places, and a ghost light lures her deeper into the house. With her ex threatening to show up again, Katja must find the courage to stand up for herself. Throw in an ol' fisherman with fatherly advice, a devilishly handsome carpenter, and witchy neighbors who like to throw something called "moon parties," Katja soon has the divorce support group of dreams.

But can a Midwestern empty-nester with no skills to call her own reinvent herself in an eccentric island town? With 44 years under her belt and nothing left to lose, Katja is about to find out.

CRONE OF COCONUT COURT, a Paranormal Women's Fiction novel about starting over in midlife, harnessing the magic within, and friendships after divorce, is Book #2 in the Dead & Breakfast series by Gabrielle Keyes.

Dear Reader,

If you enjoyed Witch of Key Lime Lane, please:

➢ leave a rating/review on Amazon and Goodreads

➢ join my READER GROUP (on Gabrielle Keyes Books website) to receive *ONE FREE MAGIC SPELL* each month, new release updates, free chapters, and giveaways!

➢ read Book 2, CRONE OF COCONUT COURT

➢ pre-order Book 3, MAGE OF MANGO ROAD

Thank you so much for your support!

- Gabrielle Keyes

GABRIELLE KEYES

ACKNOWLEDGMENTS

Switching to a new genre is hard. You never know if readers will love your new direction. I'd like to thank the following people for their help:

Jodi Turchin, Kelly Karsner Clarke, Kim Greyson, Rachel Van Fossen, and Daisy Lyle, for their astute observations and last-minute comments. Shelley Dorey and Michelle St. James, for their generous advice during my lateral move to Paranormal Women's Fiction, Murphy Nuñez for insisting I write on the schedule that works for me, not the 9-to-5 into which I kept trying to pound myself, the real-life Bowie for being my support cat, and Curtis Sponsler for a beautiful book cover, for always supporting me, whether in my career, spiritual growth, or any of my new adventures.

GABRIELLE KEYES is the Paranormal Women's Fiction pen name of Gaby Triana, bestselling horror author of 20 novels for teens and adults, including the Haunted Florida series (*Island of Bones, River of Ghosts, City of Spells*), *Wake the Hollow, Cakespell, Summer of Yesterday,* and *Paradise Island: A Sam and Colby Story.* She's a short story contributor in *Don't Turn Out the Lights: A Tribute Anthology to Alvin Schwartz's Scary Stories to Tell in the Dark*, a flash fiction contributor in *Weird Tales Magazine* Issue #365, and the host of a YouTube channel called *The Witch Haunt.*

Published with HarperCollins, Simon & Schuster, Permuted Press, and Entangled, Gaby writes about witchy powers, ghosts, haunted places, and abandoned locations. She's ghostwritten 50+ novels for bestselling authors, and her books have won IRA Teen Choice, ALA Best Paperback, and Hispanic Magazine's Good Reads Awards. She lives in Miami with her family and a gaggle of four-legged aliens, including the real-life Bowie.

Facebook: @GabrielleKeyesBooks
Instagram: @GabrielleKeyesBooks
Gabrielle Keyes Website

GABRIELLE KEYES

More Books by Gabrielle Keyes

WITCH OF KEY LIME LANE
CRONE OF COCONUT COURT
MAGE OF MANGO ROAD

Books by Gaby Triana

MOON CHILD
PARADISE ISLAND: A Sam & Colby Story
ISLAND OF BONES
RIVER OF GHOSTS
CITY OF SPELLS
CAKESPELL
WAKE THE HOLLOW
SUMMER OF YESTERDAY
RIDING THE UNIVERSE
THE TEMPTRESS FOUR
CUBANITA
BACKSTAGE PASS

Made in the USA
Coppell, TX
20 February 2022

73852174R00140